A BOY IN WAR

Jan de Groot

sononis
PRESS
WINLAW, BRITISH COLUMBIA

LIBRARY AND ARCHIVES CANADA CATALOGUING IN PUBLICATION

De Groot, Jan, 1932–
    A boy in war / Jan de Groot.

ISBN 978-1-55039-167-1

    1. De Groot, Jan, 1932- --Childhood and youth. 2. World War,
1939-1945--Children--Netherlands--Biography. 3. World War,
1939-1945--Jews--Rescue--Netherlands. 4. Netherlands--History--German
occupation, 1940-1945. 5. World War, 1939-1945--Personal narratives, Dutch.
I. Title.

DJ287.D43 2008   940.53'161092   C2008-904098-8

Sono Nis Press most gratefully acknowledges support for our publishing pro-
gram provided by the Government of Canada through the Book Publishing
Industry Development Program (BPIDP) and the Canada Council for the
Arts, and by the Province of British Columbia through the British Columbia
Arts Council and the Book Publishing Tax Credit, Ministry of Provincial
Revenue.

All photography courtesy of the de Groot family unless otherwise noted
Map by Paperglyphs
Edited by Laura Peetoom and Dawn Loewen
Cover and interior design by Jim Brennan

Published by
SONO NIS PRESS
Box 160
Winlaw, BC V0G 2J0
1-800-370-5228

books@sononis.com
www.sononis.com

Printed and bound in Canada

Distributed in the U.S. by
Orca Book Publishers
Box 468
Custer, WA 98240-0468
1-800-210-5277

The Canada Council | Le Conseil des Arts
for the Arts | du Canada

In memory of my father and mother

A Note about Pronunciation

Dutch names and terms are used throughout this story, and some readers might like to know the right way to say them. If you are one of those readers, look here for pronunciations of character names. Look at the back of the book for a longer guide to pronouncing many of the Dutch terms and place names.

Arie: "AH-rie" (with slightly rolled *r*)
Folkert: "FOAL-curt"
Frey: "fray"
Jaap: "yap"
Jan: "yahn"
Koos: "kose"
Mam (Mom): "mum"
Moeder (Mother): "MOO-der"
Oom (Uncle): "ohm"
Oma (Grandmother): "OH-ma"
Opa (Grandfather): "OH-pa"
Pa (Dad): roughly pronounced as in English
Pia: "PEE-uh"
Sjaak: "shack"
Vader (Father): "VAH-der"
Wim: "vim"

Prologue

A war on the scale of the Second World War has never been fought on North American soil. For this reason, many people in North America do not really understand what it is like to live in a country where such battles take place. The terrorist attack of September 11, 2001, although a horrifying event, pales in comparison with the destruction and death that takes place in war-torn countries. North America has been and is again at war, but while the soldiers are away fighting, the ordinary citizens—men, women, and children—are safe and secure at home, unlike the inhabitants of those countries under attack or occupied by the enemy. More than *fifty million* people died during the Second World War from 1939 to 1945, and the majority were innocent victims—not soldiers, but civilians!

I am no longer a boy. My brother passed away a few years ago and my mother died in 1994 at the age of ninety-four. Each letter she had received from my father while he was incarcerated in a concentration camp was carefully saved in a little jewellery box. As an adult, I made several attempts to read those letters. I would unfold one of them and start reading, but after a few sentences, overcome with emotion, I had to fold it again and put it back into its little box. When my mother passed away, I inherited the box with its treasured contents. Finally, I found the courage to read them. That's when I decided that it was time to share my story, the story that has been locked up in my memories for so many years.

Tens of thousands of people have their own tales. So many have lived through similar circumstances, so many children and their parents have suffered dreadfully—yet, in spite of it all, tried to live as normally as possible—in their war-torn country.

This is my story.

The
Netherlands
during the
**Second
World War**

Travels

---- By train
······ On foot

0   25 km

GRONINGEN

FRIESLAND

JOURE   HEERENVEEN
FARM
LEMMER   DRENTE

GIETHOORN
MEPPEL

STAPHORST

ZWOLLE

NOORD
HOLLAND   OVERIJSSEL

DEVENTER

AMSTERDAM

AMERSFOORT
UTRECHT   ZUTPHEN
DEN HAAG   GELDERLAND
        ZUID   UTRECHT
        HOLLAND GOUDA   ×TRAIN ON FIRE
ROTTERDAM   ARNHEM

                                    RHINE RIVER

NOORD BRABANT

ZEELAND
                EINDHOVEN

                LIMBURG   GERMANY

BELGIUM

FRANCE

1

It happened on May 10, 1940. Early in the morning, I woke up to a lot of noise echoing through the streets: the droning of engines, people running, gunshots. Suddenly, I heard the doorbell ring. It was my friend Dick.

"Come quick, the Germans are coming."

"The Germans?"

"Yes, you know, soldiers, planes. Come downstairs quick!"

Germans? Soldiers? I didn't know what he meant. Judging by his behaviour it was something very exciting. I looked around the apartment. My brother was still fast asleep, and my mother too; I guess they hadn't heard the noise. Pa wasn't home; his job had taken him away from The Hague. Hastily, I put on some clothes, left the apartment, and went downstairs. When I arrived on the ground floor, there were soldiers in the portico. Then I noticed where the engine noise came from. Above the soccer fields on the other side of the canal, above the park, and in the distance, as far as I could see, there were planes, big planes.

And there were clouds of parachutes hanging in the sky, with more dropping from the planes. Many drifted in our direction, most of them above the park and the soccer fields. The three Dutch soldiers in the portico were firing their rifles at the figures dangling from the parachutes. I noticed our soldiers were poorly dressed, their uniforms hastily put on. One wore a jacket; the other two were in shirtsleeves. Their puttees were not done up. I stared at the scene and the consternation around me. The planes, the parachutes, the soldiers shooting their rifles: it was like watching a movie. The whole thing seemed unreal.

Other people gathered in the portico—neighbours from other apartments. I heard one of the soldiers say, "The main attack is on Ockenburg, the airport, about seven kilometres from here. We had no warning, no idea this would happen. We are supposed to be neutral."

I was bewildered, wondering, "What's going on? What's happening?" I looked at Dick, who was now joined by Tonny. "Hey, Jan," they both yelled, "isn't this exciting? Isn't this fun?" Yes, I thought, exciting—but fun? I wasn't all that certain.

Before long, the battle was over. Our small army, poorly equipped, ill prepared, and surprised, could not withstand the superior force of the invaders. On May 16, the German troops moved in, their black boots pounding on the pavement. Shouting orders, they rounded up the scattered defenders, then marched them through the streets, hands in the air, disarmed, with Dick, Tonny, and I tagging along. We watched as the prisoners were loaded into waiting trucks. The Germans paid no attention to us. We were just little kids.

In some parts of Holland the small Dutch army had stood its ground and fought ferocious battles. On the whole, the Dutch army proved stronger than Hitler and his generals had expected. Rotterdam was among the cities whose defence force refused to give up. On May 14, the Germans, becoming impatient, sent in their big bomber planes and practically flattened the city, setting it aflame. We were only a little over sixteen kilometres away and could hear the devastating bombs hit their targets.

Ed Nadort, who was a few years older than I, saw it happen. He lived in Bolnes, on the outskirts of Rotterdam, and when the planes came in from the east, he and some friends had been on a back road that had an unrestricted view of the city. The planes were flying very low, so low that Ed and his friends could see the pilots waving at them. The wind blew pieces of charred paper from the burning city toward them after the bombs were dropped. The boys chased and caught some of them and tried to read what was printed through the burned areas. Ed found the front page of a Bible from the St. Laurens church, a beautiful building that had been almost completely destroyed. He told us that a few days after the bombing, he and his family could smell the stench of decaying flesh. That smell was to evoke mental pictures of the bombing for the rest of their lives.

That same night, the sky to the southeast of us lit up, as if the sun had set on the wrong side of the planet. Reports of destruction came in: the main hospital along with four others, two concert halls, twelve cinemas, five hundred cafés, twenty-five hundred stores, seventy schools, twenty-one churches…the list went on. About eight hundred people were killed and tens of thousands injured and left homeless, mainly in the poorer district of the city. As we watched in horror, seeing the glare of the fires against the sky, the tragedy and despair of our situation began to sink in. The next day, fearing further destruction, the Dutch authorities capitulated. We were now officially under control of the foreign power.

2.

Moerweg 168, The Hague, Holland. The address is located on a quiet street on the outskirts of the city. It's in one of those large and long apartment buildings, four storeys high, each building occupying an entire city block. Number 168 is on the first *étage*—the second floor—on the corner of the Moerweg and the Hadewiech Straat. The entrance is via a portico that houses a granite stairway leading to landings on each floor, two doors at each landing, one on the left and one on the right. The door on the left of the first landing is the entrance to number 168. This is where I live.

The view from these apartments along the Moerweg is unrestricted and much appreciated by the residents. The apartment blocks are on one side of the street. On the other side is a *plantsoen*, a narrow park area surrounded by a hedge, intersected with narrow pathways which lead to the Beek, one of the many canals that crisscross Holland. Across from the canal are soccer fields and beyond that a large park, called Zuiderpark. In the park are a small zoo and a pavilion with a swimming pool which I often visit because my mother likes swimming. While she swims, I am given swimming lessons by one of the instructors.

I am seven years old, the younger of two sons in the family. Folkert, my brother, is twelve years older. I guess I am a latecomer. My brother often claims that I fell off a moving van. I know he's only kidding, but we are quite different. He has dark wavy hair and is tall. I am small, with a freckled face and pale

Mam and I in 1940 or 1941.

Rudy, Tonny's little brother, watches me fishing in the Beek, c. 1942.

blond hair that looks like straw.

I am not particularly happy with our residence, which we moved to just a year ago. The portico is a great place for kids to play when it is raining, especially on the ground floor where we can hide and play marbles under the granite stairwell. But I really miss our old place, a house with a large garden around it. I feel claustrophobic in our new location, regardless of the canal, the park, and the view.

My two closest friends are Tonny, who lives in the apartment on the other side of the landing, and Dick, who lives above us. We attend the same school, we play marbles on the sidewalk, and we fish in the canal. Sometimes, we explore a strip of vacant land down the road, a swamp with lots of water. There we built a raft, put a mast on it, and rigged a bedsheet (taken from my mother's linen closet) for a sail. We float it across the open stretches pretending to be crossing the ocean, or we hide among the reeds, imagining being pirates looking for treasure. Often we roller skate or play with our scooters. But usually we hang around the canal, play with homemade toy boats, or sneak aboard the barges that are sometimes tied up along the shore.

One time, when we were playing alongside the canal, one of my toy boats drifted away in the wind. I tried to get it to come closer to the shore by throwing rocks behind it, hoping that the waves made by the rocks would push the little boat in my direction. It helped a little bit, but it still didn't come close enough. I found a stick and tried reaching for the boat. Suddenly, I fell into the water. I couldn't swim and the mild current, together with my attempts to stay afloat, made me get farther and farther away from shore. As I cried for help, big gulps of water came into my mouth, and I started to sink. I heard my friends yelling...then nothing. Suddenly, I was floating around in a space of stillness surrounded by beautiful flashing and luminous colours, red and blue, green and yellow. Then I imagined that I was lying on a hard surface. My chest was hurting. I became aware of my surroundings: I wasn't imagining! There was a man bending over me, his hands pushing on my aching chest. I coughed and threw up large amounts of water.

Apparently, Mr. Hendriks, a neighbour who had watched the commotion from his window, had come running and jumped into the water. He managed to grab me and pull me to the shore. He put me on the pathway and revived me. I was saved, but it had been a close call. After that I started swimming lessons at the park.

The Netherlands, officially called Koninkrijk der Nederlanden (Kingdom of the Netherlands) and also known as Holland, is a tiny European country. In fact, it is so small that it could easily fit inside Canada 235 times. It is bordered on the south by Belgium and on the east by Germany. The western and northern sides are coastal regions alongside the North Sea.

Holland is actually a deceptive name for the country since only two of its provinces are named Holland: South Holland and North Holland. Many people believe that Holland means "hollow land" but this is incorrect. It was originally Holt Land or Hout Land, meaning "woodland." The Netherlands means "the low lands."

At present, while Canada has a population of approximately thirty-three million, the population of the Netherlands is a little over sixteen million. In other words, while the Netherlands is not even as big as Nova Scotia, it has almost one-half the number of inhabitants as all of Canada. One would think that there wouldn't be enough room for all these people in such a small country; however, since most people are concentrated in large cities such as Amsterdam, The Hague, and Rotterdam, there are still large expanses of forested areas, lakes, and moors.

Holland was at one time a powerful seagoing nation with a large fleet of ships. Dutch merchants travelled and traded all over the world. New Zealand was named after Zeeland, one of the provinces of the Netherlands. Australia was discovered by Dutch sailors as was the route to the East Indies. Dutch merchants were the first to trade with Japan, and South Africa grew with the settlement of Dutch farmers. Dutch settlers are the reason we call people from the New York area "Yankees." Jan and Kees were, and still are, popular first names for Dutch men. Settlers in New Amsterdam (later New York) were referred to collectively as Jan-Kees, which eventually became Yan-Kees (the Dutch *j* is pronounced as the English consonant *y*), then Yankees. In New York, Harlem is named after Haarlem, a city close to Amsterdam. Flushing is named after Vlissingen, and several other cities in the state of New York also have Dutch names.

Other influences can be seen in North American culture. "Cookies" (the word, from *koekjes*) and doughnuts (the pastry, not the name) both came from the Dutch. April Fool's Day has many possible origins, but one contender comes from sixteenth-century

Holland, when the country was occupied by Spain. On April 1, 1572, a fleet of ships with rebels against Spain dropped anchor near the Dutch city of Den Briel. The city was like a fortress surrounded by walls and difficult to capture. The admiral of the fleet learned that the main force of the Spanish occupiers had left the city to fight a battle elsewhere. He fooled the remaining defenders into believing that his attackers were a force of five thousand, when they were actually only eleven hundred. This foolery caused panic and chaos in the city, allowing the rebels to reclaim it for the Dutch in the name of William of Orange. The event led to the beginning of the retreat of the Spanish from Dutch territory, and to this day it is celebrated in Holland each April 1. As Dutch settlers spread throughout the world, their April 1 foolery became an international event.

Then there is Santa Claus. Saint Nicholas, in Holland referred to as Sint Nikolaas or Sinterklaas, was a Greek nobleman who has been credited with many good deeds, especially for the poor. He became a bishop in Myra (now Demre), Turkey, and subsequently a Christian saint whose life is celebrated in many countries, usually on December 6. In Holland, the feast of Saint Nicholas is celebrated the evening before, on December 5, with the giving of gifts and candy. It's still a very popular occasion that begins in November, when Sint Nikolaas, a stately, white-bearded man dressed in the red robes of a Roman Catholic bishop, arrives by steamboat from Spain. In the 1860s, Thomas Nast, a New York cartoonist, took the tall and stately Sinterklaas, mixed him up with English and Scandinavian Christmas characters, added a sled and some reindeer, and turned him into that short, fat, jolly icon of Christmas, Santa Claus.

At the beginning of the twentieth century, the Dutch were keeping themselves busy building dikes and reclaiming land from the sea, using their well-known windmills to pump water from areas where dikes had been constructed. The kingdom of the Netherlands was still prosperous, with several colonies: Indonesia,

Suriname, and several islands in the Caribbean. It got along well with its close neighbours, Germany and Belgium; during the First World War, from 1914 to 1918, Holland stayed out of the conflict and was declared neutral territory.

So, when again Germany raised the spectre of war, this time under the command of Adolf Hitler, everyone believed that Holland would again be neutral. Everyone knew Germany would not attack Holland—they were friends! No one expected invasion, capitulation, and subsequent occupation. But it came, to everyone's surprise and horror.

3

The fear and unrest slowly started to settle down as we adjusted to the presence of the occupying forces. We kids continued with most of our usual activities of school and play, although cautiously.

The end of the Moerweg was only a few blocks away from our building. The road became a path that led to a forest called Overvoorde, another favourite area for us to explore. A few months into the occupation we could no longer play there because the Germans had surrounded it with rolls of barbed wire. They scattered land mines along the perimeter and erected signs that said *Betreten verboten!* (Entrance forbidden!) A sentry stood at the entrance at all times. One of the soldiers standing guard let it slip to us that deep inside the forest a launching pad for rockets was being built. The rockets were to be used to destroy England, that so-called evil country across the North Sea. I was miffed by the word "evil," because I had gone to England on a few occasions with our sailboat and had quite enjoyed our visits there.

My father was in the police force. He joined in The Hague in 1919. Eight years later, on May 25, 1927, he and his partner, Pieter van Veenendaal, were commended for their good police work and heroic behaviour leading to the arrest of two people involved in auto theft. One day, Mam proudly showed me the commendation, written and signed by the chief of police. Looking back, I guess he must have been some sort of detective. Many years ago, he had also had something to do with the palace. I was told that in

My father (Folkert de Groot Sr.), in civilian clothes, surrounded by his uniformed colleagues, 1942.

those days he often went away with Prince Hendrik, the husband of Queen Wilhelmina. It was rumoured that Prince Hendrik had some lady friends and that my father had helped him cover his tracks. I overheard one of my aunts complain about this to my uncle; apparently it had been mentioned in the newspapers. She seemed to be annoyed about my father's involvement.

At the time of the invasion Pa was working not only in The Hague, but also in other places, sometimes travelling to other countries. I had heard him mention ICPC, which stood for International Criminal Police Commission. (Later it became known as Interpol.) He had a uniform with lots of silver things and buttons on it, but he rarely wore it. I remember him best in his nice grey suit and felt hat.

Every year, Mam and Pa went on a long trip: vacations in France, Italy, and Switzerland. But that was before the war started. Now they didn't go anywhere anymore. My father still occasionally went away, but not, according to my mother, on official police

Mam and Pa on the Matchless with me tucked in between, 1938.

business. "It's a secret," she would say, and we, my brother and I, were not allowed to mention it to anyone.

My father liked motorcycles. He had an Indian, then an Ariels, and then a Matchless. I remember them well, especially the Matchless. It was black with lots of chrome and it had a sidecar. He used to take me for rides in it. Sometimes Dick and Tonny went along too. Two of us would sit in the sidecar, and the third sat on the back of the motorcycle, holding on to my father.

Pa's latest motorcycle was a Harley-Davidson with huge handlebars. Once the war started it was hidden in my bedroom, because it was illegal to own such a machine. All motorcycles and cars were confiscated by the Germans. Later on, they took bicycles—or just bicycle tires. The Germans needed the rubber for their trucks and other vehicles.

In August 1940, we had been occupied for three months. It was my eighth birthday and it was turning into the best one ever. Pa told me to go outside and wait for a surprise. I had no idea what was going to happen. Tonny and Dick and I, plus a few other friends, were waiting on the sidewalk in front of the portico. To pass the time we played with our marbles, trying to shoot them into the pot, a small cavity we made in the pavement. A blue marble was worth ten points, red, twenty points, and yellow, thirty. Each player started with an equal number of points. The first one to shoot all the marbles into the pot was the winner and got to keep them all. We were waiting for Pa to call us, to let us know when the surprise was ready. He still hadn't called; we waited and waited and waited.

Suddenly a delivery van drove up and stopped in front of the portico. Two men jumped from the van, opened the back door and started to pull on something. That piqued our interest: something to keep us occupied while waiting for Pa's call. We collected the marbles and gathered around the back of the van.

"Move away, boys," one of the men said. "Give us some room to unload this thing."

The other man was studying a piece of paper.

"Are you certain this is the right address?" asked the man who had told us to move.

"Yup, got it right here, Moerweg 168."

That caught my attention. That was my address. What could they be delivering? Something so big that it had to be brought with a moving van? I tried to look inside. There were several items, most of them in crates. On the floor, in the middle, there was this long thing. One of the men jumped in and started to lift it, while the other pulled on the other end from street level. It was wrapped in blankets. They pulled it from the van and set it down on the sidewalk. One of the men went upstairs and rang the doorbell at 168. The other started to remove the blankets, which apparently belonged to the movers. Fascinated, we watched as the object

My *kano*, 1940. Left to right: unknown, me, Rudy (Tonny's brother), Henk van der Meiden, unknown, Folkert (my brother).

began to appear. It was a *kano*, a Dutch watercraft that looks and is operated much like a kayak. This particular *kano* was a sailing kind with a centreboard, a mast and sail, and a detachable rudder. It was the most beautiful *kano* we had ever seen. Gleaming with white paint and a brightly varnished cockpit coaming, it sparkled in the sun.

I was so entranced by its beauty that I had not noticed my father coming down the stairs. Suddenly, there he was. He inspected the *kano*, signed the form that the delivery man presented to him, and said, "You can leave it here. The rest is up to the owner." Then he turned to me and said, "Well, what do you think of it?"

I looked at him, then at the *kano*, and then back at him. I didn't know what to say. Was this for real? No, it couldn't be.

"Well?" Pa said again. "What do you think of it? Happy birthday!"

I could not believe my ears. This most fantastic, this most

gorgeous, this stunning, best-looking *kano* I had ever seen, was mine, mine, mine! I jumped up and down, I screamed, I yelled, I rolled on the pavement. Along with my friends, I touched and stroked this incredible birthday present.

Pa laughed, watching our antics. "I take it you are pleased with it, then?"

"Oh, yes, Vader, it's the best, the bestest, birthday I've ever had, thank you, thank you." I embraced him and Mam, who had joined the party. My brother, who had also appeared, was inspecting the centreboard, the mast, the sail, the paddles, and was fitting the pintles of the rudder into the gudgeons at the stern. He pulled on the cord to test the vertical movement of the rudder blade. "It all seems to be working fine," he said, reporting to my father. "Shall we give it a try?"

"Ask your brother," Pa answered. "It's his *kano*."

He didn't have to ask me—I was ready to go. With my father at the bow and Folkert at the stern, the *kano* was lifted, Dick and Tonny and I and the others all giving a helping hand. That wasn't really necessary, as the *kano* was light and easily carried by two grown-ups. But we couldn't keep our hands off it, so the craft was rapidly moved to the canal and launched. There was room for two adults or four little guys like us. All day long, we paddled that *kano*; we tried sailing, but there was no wind. It was getting dark when my father called us and said it was time to call it a day. The *kano* was hauled out of the water and put to rest on top of the *schuur*, a storage locker behind the apartment, where, unbeknownst to me, my father and brother had made a little shelter in which the *kano* fit perfectly.

That evening I learned that the *kano* had been a little conspiracy among my father, my grandfather, and Folkert, its construction planned several months earlier. The *kano* had been built in my grandfather's shipyard up north.

4

The Beek flowed past the forest where the rocket launch was being constructed. This canal skirted the forest boundaries and eventually ended up in an area called the Westland. That area was almost completely covered with greenhouses and vegetable fields. Grapes, cucumbers, and tomatoes were grown in the greenhouses. The fields were planted mainly with potatoes, but also with leeks, carrots, lettuce, and other vegetables. The region was famous as a major supplier of produce to much of Europe. Now it was under heavy guard by the Germans, with the produce used to feed the German army.

But the fields were guarded from the road, not from the water side—no obstacle to three little boys and a *kano*. We would paddle or sail down the canal until we reached the fields, not worrying about being spotted, since no one paid much attention to little boys. We would hide the *kano* in the tall reeds that grew alongside the banks of the canal, jump out with our burlap bags, and fill them with whatever we wanted: potatoes, carrots, lettuce, sugar beets.

One day, while out in the *kano*, we saw a British fighter plane crash in one of the fields. The pilot had jumped out and was floating down in a parachute. The plane had been hit by German anti-aircraft guns. Dick and I berthed the *kano*; Tonny wasn't with us at the time. We ran to the site of the crash; we wanted to see the plane. The pilot had drifted away, somewhere in the distance. When we got there, we heard men shouting and shots being fired. The Germans were moving toward the plane too, but from the opposite direction. They spotted us and didn't want us there. They came after us. We ran as fast as we could. Suddenly we came upon a *sloot*, an irrigation ditch. It was deep and wide and full of water; it seemed too wide for us to jump across. But we had no choice, no time to think. This was not a game, not a contest...we feared for our lives! So we jumped.

Somehow Dick and I made it across with room to spare. When I looked behind me, still running, I saw two German soldiers standing on the other side of the ditch, unwilling to jump. Maybe the ditch was too wide for them; we could never have cleared it if we hadn't been so scared. They shot a few bullets as we kept running, to scare us off, I guess. They gave up the chase and we found our way back to the *kano*.

A few days later, to my surprise, we received a guest in the house. He arrived late in the evening. Two other men were with him. They talked to my father for a few minutes and then left. It all seemed a bit mysterious. The man who stayed spoke English. Then I heard that he was the pilot of the plane that had crashed. He was going to stay with us for a while until arrangements could be made for his transport to a safe destination. Switzerland was the word I heard mentioned. After I had been introduced to him, my father took me aside.

"Listen carefully, Jan. Our house is what is called a 'safe house.' That means that sometimes we will have people staying with us who are hiding from the Nazis. We must keep this a secret. Nobody must know about this, not even your friends, Dick and Tonny—nobody! Now, I know I can trust you, so promise you won't ever, ever tell anybody about this. Agreed? Also, when we have people staying here, you cannot invite any of your friends into the house, or they'll find out what's happening here and tell others who may become suspicious. Do you understand?"

"Yes, Vader, I understand, I promise. I'll never tell anybody about this, and I'll think of some excuse when Dick and Tonny want to come over."

"That's my boy," Pa said, giving me a hug. "I knew I could count on you."

The pilot was in his late twenties. I tried to start a conversation with him but he couldn't speak Dutch and I couldn't speak English. We ended up looking at each other, the pilot nodding his head every once in a while, giving me a smile. He seemed nervous and was probably worried about what would happen to him. Mam tried to make him relax and gave him a cup of tea, but every time there was a noise outside from a passing car or truck, he would stand up from his chair, look nervously around the room and then watch the door as if he expected someone to come in. I fetched a sketchbook and with a pencil drew a plane on it. He nodded, then took the pencil and started to perfect it. In the cockpit he drew the head of a person. He pointed at it and then pointed at himself. "Pilot," he said. I nodded and also said "Pilot," pointing at him and the person in the plane, meaning that I understood. He stayed with us for three days, until the same two men who had brought him came to take him away.

From then on, whenever we had "guests" (which happened more frequently as time went on), I told my friends that my mother was ill, or my brother had some contagious disease, or whatever excuse I could think of. Somehow it worked and they never argued.

For my father, my promise of silence must have been something to worry about. What eight-year-old boy could be trusted to keep such a secret and to resist the urge to brag about it to his friends? But I never felt such an urge. The war was changing everything and everyone.

Our apartment had a large storage room, where the gas and electrical meters were located. My father and Folkert changed it into a small storage room by building a wall across the back of it. The walled-off area became a small, separate room, whose entrance was hidden in the back wall of the rear bedroom closet. Whenever the doorbell rang, our guests went into this secret room and stayed there until it was safe to come out.

My brother was a talented fellow. He had a degree in art and was employed as a commercial artist by a company that designed displays for cinemas, with drawings and paintings of the featured stars. He also worked for the Bijenkorf, a department store, designing displays and advertisements. In addition, he was an excellent pianist. Sometimes he played at the Metropole theatre accompanying silent movies, or during intermission.

At home we had a giant grand piano my parents bought for Folkert. My mother played piano as well, and I was also taught to play. My teacher was Mr. Geenjaar. He came once a week and gave me lessons: exercises, scales, and complicated pieces by Czerny and Schmidt, which later I had to practise. When I practised the exercises, my mother usually sat beside me, counting the beat by tapping her fingers on the edge of the keyboard. When I made a mistake, she gave me a poke and told me to start again.

I didn't like to practise, especially on a nice day when my friends were playing outside. But I enjoyed listening to my brother playing, even more so when some of his buddies came over with their trumpet, bass, drums, and violin. They played jazz, the whole place swinging and full of good, happy feelings.

We needed happy feelings as the Germans' grip on our lives grew tighter. With so much being shipped out to feed the German army, food for us was becoming more scarce. The government issued ration tickets to make sure everyone got a fair share of the available food. They looked like a sheet of postage stamps. Each day, it was announced in the newspaper which numbers were valid and for what kind of food. People would line up to receive their allotted portions—so much sugar, bread, cooking oil, and so on per person. We didn't do too badly because my brother used his talent to forge each day's numbers on our tickets. Then he gave me one and I went to the store to use it. It had to be me, because I was a small kid. If the forgery was detected, I was asked, "Where did you get this?" Then I would play dumb and say that I had found it lying in the street. They believed me because they didn't think that I was capable of forging it myself. I would get off with a reprimand, whereas an adult would have been arrested immediately and shipped off to Germany.

My brother also removed the letter *J* from identification cards. Every night he did several. Bunches of those cards were delivered regularly. They belonged to Jews.

This thing about Jews I couldn't understand. What was a Jew? What made a Jew different from other people? I asked Mam about it. She said, "Jewish people have a different religion. They are Jewish."

"Is that bad?" I asked.

"No, of course not, but the Germans say it is."

"So what if you are a Catholic, or a Protestant like Oma and Opa?"

"I guess that's okay, because the Germans are not pursuing Catholics and Protestants."

"But there was a boy in school who said that he was Jewish and yet he and his family went to a Protestant church. How can he be Jewish and Protestant at the same time?"

Mam thought for a minute, and then she said, "Jewish people come from a different country, so even if they are Protestant they are still Jewish."

"But he didn't come from a different country. He was Dutch. He spoke Dutch just like us, and he was born in Holland and as far as I know, he didn't even have any relatives in foreign countries. So how could he be Dutch and Jewish at the same time?"

"You bring up an interesting question," Mam said. "I don't have a clear answer for it. Actually, I don't understand it either." Then, changing the subject, she asked, "Where is that boy now?"

A portrait of my mother, Alida de Groot-Weydom (1918).

"I don't know. He's no longer in school."

"Hmm. He was probably sent to a camp in Germany, or perhaps is hiding somewhere. I hope he's okay."

Gradually, over two years of occupation, the Germans tightened the reins: curfews, more restrictions, stricter rules. Jewish people were now in great danger; when found, they were being carted off to concentration camps.

Not only Jews were being taken, however. One day my brother did not come home. Someone from his place of work told my mother that he had been arrested and transported to Germany. Not because he had done anything illegal; no, it was just that he was old enough to work in a factory there. Several of his friends were taken too. When Pa was told, he didn't say much, but I could tell by the expression on his face that he was shocked and very, very sad. Mam was devastated and cried. I cried too. I missed my big brother a lot. The place seemed empty without him. Now there would be no more music, no bass, violin, and trumpet, no jazz...no more happy feelings.

5

In the fall of 1942, my father became a hero. The official police report described the incident something like this. On Saturday, September 26, 1942, at about 1530 hours, Folkert de Groot had been on his bicycle in the area of the Z.W.B. Singel, The Hague, which borders a canal. At the time he was off duty and was wearing civilian clothes. Near the tax office he spotted a small crowd of people and heard cries for help. When he approached, he noticed a boy of approximately age nine struggling and sinking in the water. Since there were no other rescue aids available, he immediately took off his overcoat and jumped fully dressed into the water, landing right where the child had disappeared beneath the water's surface. He managed to find and grab the boy and with great difficulty, because of his clothing and the hernia brace he was wearing, pulled him to shore, where onlookers helped both of them from the chilly water. He himself had come to no harm, but his suit and watch had suffered some damage.

The police report was broadcast over the radio and appeared in all the local newspapers in complete detail, including the names, ages, and addresses of everyone involved—the boy, several witnesses, and my father. Pa was furious. "How did they get hold of that report, and why are they making such a big fuss about it? When Hendriks pulled Jan out of the water no one made any mention of it," he complained.

As a token of appreciation, the boy's parents gave my father a beautiful diamond tie pin. Pa didn't want to accept it, but they insisted. Since Pa didn't wear that kind of jewellery, he had it made into a ring for my mother. While he was very happy with the outcome of his adventure (the boy was alive and well), he was worried that all the publicity would draw attention to the illegal activities he was involved in. However, after a few days of turning away the reporters who knocked at the door, things settled down, and no harm was done.

I had an experience that made me feel like a bit of a hero, too. Marbles—*knikkers*, it's called in Dutch—was one of the games I was really good at. Actually, I guess I was a bit of a shark at this game. Most of the kids who knew me didn't want to play with me because I usually won—which meant I took home all of their marbles. So, often on my way to school on my roller skates, I carried a bag of marbles, looking for marble players who didn't know me. One day I spotted some, five of them, shooting from the curb. Two of them were also on roller skates. I stopped to watch for a while and then, showing my bag of marbles, I said, "Can I play too?"

"Sure," they agreed. "We're just about to start a new game."

It didn't take long for them to find out they were no match for my well-honed skills. I rapidly made the right moves and was just about to grab the marbles from the pot when one of them got angry and yelled, "Hands off! Those are my marbles."

He was a big fellow, much bigger than I. He came at me with his fists ready. I was scared, but not scared enough to make me abandon my winnings. I quickly grabbed the marbles before taking off on my roller skates. Fortunately, he wasn't wearing skates and couldn't keep up with me. After a short pursuit he gave up.

After that I stayed away from the area, so as not to run into him. But suddenly, three days later on another street, there he was right in front of me, appearing out of nowhere. No chance to escape this time. The big fellow grabbed my jacket and pulled, then pushed me. I fell over backwards and he stood over me, one leg on each side. He was about to punch me in the face when I remembered a trick my father had taught me. Pa sometimes taught my brother and me jiu-jitsu, and the situation I was in now was exactly like one I had rehearsed several times. I quickly grabbed the big fellow's ankles, brought my knees up between his legs, and put them against his knees. With a bit of quick pressure, the fellow lost his balance and fell over backwards. I quickly stood up beside him and raised my fists. To my surprise, he curled up, holding his hands over his face.

"Don't hit me, please, don't hit me," he begged.

I stood up and straightened my jacket. Full of confidence and feeling two feet taller, I said, "You stay out of my way from now on, you hear? Next time I won't let you off this easy." I turned around and went on my way, exulting in my triumph. Thanks to my father, from that time on, I didn't have to worry about the guy. He avoided me like the plague.

In our kitchen was a big coal-burning stove with an oven. Besides being used for cooking, it also made the kitchen nice and warm. It had a compartment filled with hot water that my mother used to wash the dishes.

Saturday was laundry day. Mam put a big tub filled with water, soap, and dirty laundry on the stove and left it there, boiling. Occasionally she stirred it to make certain the garments were thoroughly soaked. After a while, she moved the tub onto the balcony, mounted a wringer on the side of it and put the washboard in. Then, the work began.

One by one, each piece of laundry was pulled from the tub and scrubbed on the washboard. Then it was put through the wringer and dumped into another tub filled with clean water. Often, I turned the wringer while Mam fed each piece through. When the laundry tub was empty, the soapy water was dumped and the wringer moved to the other tub where the laundry had received

Laundry wringer with washboard and tubs.

its rinse. There it was turned through the wringer again, and then each piece was hung up on the clothesline with clothespins, to flap and dry in the wind.

My father had suggested several times that we get a cleaning lady to help with these chores, but Mam refused each time.

"No," she would say. "This is only a small household and I can easily take care of it myself. It's a waste of money, and besides, I don't like strangers going through my things." Her refusal had probably been a good thing, because now, with people sometimes staying with us, a cleaning lady in the house would have compromised our secrecy. For this same reason my piano lessons with Mr. Geenjaar were stopped.

The stove was my mother's pride and joy. It was finished with a dark blue, baked-on enamel, beautifully decorated with flowers of many different colours accented with gold and silver. There was also a lot of chrome trim. The stove was thoroughly cleaned and polished on a regular basis; sometimes, when Mam was busy with other things, I did the polishing. Then my mother gave me a two-and-a-half-cent coin.

Dick got a similar amount when he did chores in his house. With our coins we would go to the Toko, a candy store on the way to school. Dick never spent all of his money. The half-penny in change he received he added to the others he had saved from previous visits to the Toko. I usually spent the whole coin on two *tover ballen* (magic balls) and a bar of chocolate. The *tover ballen* were large, about three centimetres in diameter. They kept changing their colour as you sucked on them: blue, red, yellow, green, purple, and eventually, when they had become very small, white. In addition to being magic, they were delicious.

About a thirty-minute walk from where we lived there was a theatre that showed movies for kids. It was quite popular. A ticket to the theatre cost ten cents, which was a lot; but sometimes, when we could get the money from our parents, Dick and I went there.

The place was small, seating about eighty—just a large room, really. The owner stood beside the projector, which was on the floor in the back. As the reel ran, the man described what was happening and what the characters were saying. He often interrupted himself to shout at someone in the audience to be quiet or to sit down. The movies were usually about pirates or ghosts, and were full of action, which of course created lots of reaction from the audience. Often, things got a little bit out of control, especially when the audience got so caught up in the story that they started yelling and shouting advice (and sometimes rude comments) to the characters in the story. Then the man stopped the projector, walked over to the culprits and told them that if they didn't behave, they would have to leave. Dick and I often found the altercations between the operator and the excited crowd even more entertaining than the movie on the screen.

But this was now all in the past. The movie place closed; the man who operated it had been taken to a concentration camp. He was a Jew. The Toko, too, was closed; *tover ballen* and chocolate bars were no longer available.

The school I attended also closed down: not enough teachers. Several of them had been sent to Germany. Another reason for school closures was to conserve electricity and heating fuel. Electricity and gas were derived from coal which, because of the war, was becoming very scarce.

Dick was one year older and Tonny was two years older than I. They were moved to one school, and I to another. I liked my new school better. It was close to the Laak, a big canal with a marina and a small shipyard. The Laak also had access to a large wholesale produce market where trucks came to haul away the vegetables brought in by the barges. There was lots of traffic on this canal and barges often tied up close to the school.

At the new school I became friends with Wim van Weenen. Wim was taller than I and he had blond curly hair. We laughed a lot and played a lot, especially on the barges. One day, during recess, Wim and I and some other boys spotted a barge lying alongside the quay. The bargemen were nowhere to be seen. We all climbed on board and started to inspect our new playground. One of the boys cast off first one mooring line, then another, and soon we were adrift. Wim and I operated the big tiller as the barge picked up a bit of current and started to move. People on shore saw us and shouted. Police arrived and with a small tug the barge was pushed back into its place. We were hustled into a waiting police van and delivered to the police station. A sergeant asked our names and wrote them in a book. When it was my turn, he put his pen down, sat back in his chair, and said, "Ah, this must have been your idea!"

"No, sir, it just sort of happened."

"It just sort of happened? You were at the tiller."

"Yes, but the barge was loose and—"

"Never mind! If you were steering you must have been the main culprit. You come with me, young man; I think I know someone who would like to have a little talk with you."

With this he got out of his chair, picked up a bunch of keys, and opened a door that led to a corridor with rows of doors on both sides. High up in each door was a little opening with a sliding panel. "These are cells," the sergeant said. He stopped in front of one of the doors, slid the panel sideways, and looked inside. "This one is empty," he said, unlocking the door. Pushing me inside, he said, "This is where we put bad little boys." He left and the door closed behind him.

In the cell was a wooden seat and a small window with bars, high up—too high for me to reach. I couldn't see what was on the other side. A bit of sunlight came through it. I sat down on the wooden bench to contemplate my predicament. I began to cry. What was going to happen to me now? Would I be in this place forever? Was this a jail? Would they ship me to Germany, just like my brother?

A clang at the door brought me back to the present. The door opened and someone came in, not in uniform. Hesitantly, I looked up. It was my father!

He looked at me sternly. "Stealing barges now, are we?"

"No, Vader, we weren't stealing, just playing," I said, wiping the tears from my face.

His face softened and he sat down next to me. He put his arm around my shoulders. "It's okay," he said. "I think you've learned your lesson. Stay away from the barges from now on. They are too dangerous, anyhow. What if you fell into the water and got caught underneath? Come, let's go home."

I grabbed his hand and we walked out of the cell. The sergeant winked as we passed his desk. Outside, a police car was waiting. My father opened the door, guided me into the passenger seat, and said to the driver, "Please take him back to his school."

"Yes, sir," said the driver, touching his hat.

"I'll see you later, Jan. Stay out of trouble."

The policeman started the engine and we drove off. When we arrived at the school, the other boys were already there and anxious to find out what had happened to me. "Was it a real cell? Did it have bars? Were there other prisoners? Were they murderers? Were you interrogated? Did they feed you bread and water?"

I filled them in on the details, exaggerating a bit. I became the hero of the day. When I came home from school not another word was spoken about the incident. But that night I had some pretty bad dreams.

We hadn't heard from my brother ever since he had been arrested and shipped off to Germany. We constantly wondered and worried about him. Then some months later (it seemed like forever), we received a letter. It was from my brother! Pa quickly opened it and read the contents out loud. He said he was doing fine. The manager of the factory where he was put to work had found out that he was a commercial artist and put him in the art department. He was now designing logos and things for the company. He figured he'd be home soon. My father's face showed a skeptical frown as he threw the letter on the table. Mam grabbed it and held it to her bosom. With her eyes closed she said, "Thank goodness, he is still alive!"

Early in 1943, we went on a short vacation in our sailboat—my father's pride and joy. When we first got it, through my grandfather, it was in poor shape, but after many days of hard work, Pa and Folkert had put it back into pristine condition. I had also put quite a bit of work into the project. I did a lot of sanding and helped wherever needed. The boat used to be kept in nearby Scheveningen, from where we sailed on the North Sea and sometimes on to the Wadden Sea. A few times we had crossed the North Sea and had gone to England. That was no longer possible, so Pa had had the boat moved to a lake called Brasemer Meer.

The boat was a little big for that kind of water; it was fourteen metres long and had a deep keel which sometimes caused us to run aground. Then we had to heel it over, which was quite a job. It took a lot of pulling on a halyard that came from the top of the mast. This could be done only with help from others and another boat. The other boat needed to be anchored some distance away from us. Then, from the other boat, we would pull on the halyard with all our might to make our boat heel sufficiently for the keel to lift from the bottom.

Our trip lasted only a few days. The weather wasn't good; there was lots of rain and it was cold. Mam decided that she'd had enough and wanted to go back home. I had a good time, though. I loved being on the boat, regardless of the weather, although this time it wasn't the same. My brother wasn't with us.

On March 21, 1943, the doorbell rang. My mother was in the kitchen; I heard her go to the door and open it. I heard her scream! I ran to the door and...there was my brother, hugging Mam! I jumped for joy. He let me drag him into the living room. He sat down in a chair, Mam too, and spellbound we listened to his story.

In the art department of the factory he'd had access to the tools he needed to make himself a permit to travel and other documents that gave him permission to be in Holland legally. The papers were signed by important German authorities—their signatures forged, of course.

6

We were glad my brother was back—but we were worried. One had to be so careful now. One of our neighbours, Mr. Wolbeer, had joined the NSB, the National Socialist Party. He now worked for the Nazis—and he was not the only one. Mr. Wolbeer wore a band with a swastika on his sleeve, but not all Nazi sympathizers did. Not being sure whom we could trust, we trusted no one, not even neighbours and friends. You never knew what might happen, who might point the finger at you. Wim and I went to the cinema to watch a movie. It was interrupted by a speech from Adolf Hitler. Two people didn't stand up to show their respect while the Führer was talking on the screen. A man who had been seated behind the twosome tapped them on the shoulder and arrested them. They were marched out of the cinema and hauled off to jail.

With all these worries, it was lucky that Wim and I had a distraction. Most Saturdays I went with my mother to the market, even though there was not much to be had there. Very few stalls were left. Still, Mam would pick through some of the goods and often bought something, usually flowers. I liked going to the market because there was a puppet theatre there. One day, Wim came with us. While my mother did her shopping, we watched the antics of the puppets, laughing and shouting as the puppeteer encouraged the audience to participate in the dialogue.

"I have a puppet theatre too, you know," I said to Wim. "My

brother and my father made it for me, and I have a whole bunch of puppets: Jan Klaassen, Katrijntje, the Policeman, the King, the Queen, and several others."

"You do? Really?"

"Sure, it's lots of fun. I'll show you next time you're over at my place."

At the time, we had no one staying at the house, so the following Sunday Wim came home with me and we immediately started to assemble the puppet theatre. I showed him how to operate the puppets, and we practised the various moves. Wim picked up on it immediately and soon we had a little bit of a play going.

We practised regularly after that, putting together a couple of stories which we then performed with the puppets. We set up outside, in the portico, and started performing for an audience of kids from the neighbourhood. The word spread and our audience grew. Then we received invitations to play at kids' birthday parties. We outgrew our small puppet theatre and together we built a larger one: wider, to give us more room, and higher so that we could stand up instead of having to crouch down all the time. We also made scenery for the stage, three-dimensional instead of just a single backdrop. For a forest we cut out shapes of trees and hung them from the top at various distances so that the puppets could move in between or behind them. Wim decided we should have lighting, too, and had his father, who was an electrical engineer, rig the theatre with lights of different colours and install a switch panel that allowed us to create special effects.

We became more creative as we gained experience. We kept a pet mouse and a salamander. When the wicked witch, one of the main characters, cast a spell on Jan Klaassen, the lights were turned off. In the sudden darkness we quickly switched Jan Klaassen for the mouse or the salamander. When the lights flickered and then stayed on, there was an animal where Jan Klassen had been. The "transformation" was accompanied by the rattling of a large, thin metal plate, to represent thunder. This trick elicited lots of oohs and aahs from our audience.

As time went on, we developed quite a nice little business. We performed regularly and were getting paid for it!

Our teacher, Mr. Boon, believed that proper use of language was the most important thing for kids to learn: to be able to express themselves, to read, to write, to communicate. He said things like, "Once you really know your own language, it is that much easier to learn foreign languages." And: "Well-spoken people get further in life." A lot of time was spent on grammar. "Proper grammar," he said, "is the most important thing about the study of language." Although normally about an hour was set aside each day for this subject, Mr. Boon usually expanded it to several hours.

Somehow he heard about our puppet theatre and asked us to give a demonstration in school. A few days later Wim and I put on our best performance. When the play ended, Mr. Boon asked us all kinds of questions about how our theatre worked. He looked inside, measured the working space, and looked at the puppets. He picked one up and put his fingers in it; the thumb into the left arm, the index finger into the head, and the middle finger into the right arm. He had some difficulty getting his fingers inside because the puppets were made for small kids. But he got the idea and went through the motions of bringing the puppet to life.

The next day, standing in front of the class, he announced that each student was to write a play. The best one would be selected and performed in a puppet theatre to be built especially for the occasion. The school would build the theatre, a large one with enough room to accommodate several kids at a time. He had spoken with the art teacher and they had come up with a way of making puppets large enough to be seen by a school audience. The heads were to be made of papier mâché, formed and glued over a core of toilet paper rolls. He would ask the mothers of the students to make the clothing. Wim and I were to act as special advisors. Our enthusiasm increased as he was speaking. This was something the whole class could participate in.

Over a couple of months, everyone wrote and submitted their plays. Each was read and evaluated in front of the class. Wim and I worked together on two plays, one of them a musical. For this we composed the music, wrote the lyrics, and then sang them while I also accompanied on the piano. Our two plays and one submitted by a classmate by the name of Appie Deurloo made it to the finals. Mr. Boon scratched his head; he was having difficulty making a choice. Finally, he announced: "We will rehearse all three of them!"

It took months to make the theatre and puppets and to rehearse the plays. At last Mr. Boon declared us ready. "We'll give our first performance next Friday in the gym," he said. "The whole school will be there to watch."

We performed the plays, and all three were a great success.

Not long after he returned, my brother got himself a girlfriend. Her name was Frey. The first time he brought her home, I fell instantly in love. She was the most beautiful girl I had ever seen, with long black curly hair, right down past her shoulders, a face like an angel, eyes that twinkled like the stars, and a smile that made me melt. My father liked her too and she got on with my mother like a house on fire. I sat and stared at her in admiration. When I gathered some courage I grabbed her hand and dragged her off to show her our puppet theatre. She was really interested, especially in the puppets' clothing. She told me she was a seamstress and made fancy dresses for very wealthy people. I told her about the puppets at school and she offered to do some sewing if we needed it. Then I told her about my *kano* and we went to the *schuur* to see it. She loved it, and asked if she could come with me sometime. "Of course," I said. "When?" We decided to meet the next Saturday morning.

Then my brother came to take her away. "That's enough," he said to me. "She's my girlfriend, you know, not yours. Go on and get your own." Laughing, they both walked away. Frey waved, calling, "See you on Saturday. Don't forget we have a date!"

Forget? How could I forget?

It seemed like eternity waiting for Saturday to arrive. Folkert helped me launch the *kano* and I had it ready and waiting well before Frey arrived.

"Maybe I should come too," Folkert said when Frey and I had settled into our seats.

"Not on your life," Frey answered. "I made this date with your brother, not with you." She promptly pushed the paddle against the shore and we were off.

"What time will you be back?" my brother yelled as we moved farther away.

"Not for a while," Frey said as she held up a paper bag. "I brought lunch!"

Soon Folkert was out of sight. A light breeze came up, and I lowered the centreboard a bit and raised the sail. We cruised down the canal.

Judging by the looks from other, more mature, male boaters, I could tell that I wasn't the only one who thought that Frey was a beautiful woman. Many came close enough to make a comment or start a conversation. One fellow who paddled frantically to keep up with us (since the wind was now pushing us along nicely) pretended to take an interest in my *kano*. Looking at Frey he said, "That's a very nice looking *kano*. What make is it?"

"It's not mine," Frey answered. "You'll have to ask him." She pointed at me.

He now looked at me and repeated his question. Proudly, I told him that it had been built in my grandfather's shipyard.

"Wow," he said, "that's great. Do you and your sister go out in it often?"

"She's not my sister," I replied. "She's my brother's girlfriend."

"Oh," he answered, obviously disappointed. "I see. Well, have a good day." He promptly stopped paddling and fell behind.

"That got rid of him in a hurry," Frey remarked.

We both laughed.

We passed Overvoorde, the forest, and were approaching the fields near the Westland. Before Overvoorde, there had been a path on both sides of the canal. The paths were used by the men who pushed the barges that had no engines. Each barge had an opening, a slot, in both the fore and aft decks. The bargemen slid their long, heavy poles into one of these slots. Sometimes poles were used fore and aft and there were usually two bargemen to a pole.

Now there was a path on only one side of the canal. The wind had died and we paddled along leisurely as the canal wound its way through the countryside. Tall reeds lined the shore on both sides. Water lilies, white, pink, and yellow, popped their heads from between large, green, saucer-shaped leaves that floated alongside the outskirts of the reeds. The ducks, busy exploring this water wonderland, seemed undisturbed by our presence. Silently we drifted along, both of us fascinated by the spectacle around us. Frey pointed to a large frog sitting on a leaf. With a croak it leapt into the water and disappeared beneath the surface.

"I had no idea this was so close to our neighbourhood," whispered Frey. "Do you come here often?"

"Yes," I answered. "Farther along is the Westland. That's where all the greenhouses are. These fields here are still bare and mostly used for cows, although I haven't seen any for a long time."

"Confined, or else moved by the Germans, I guess," Frey suggested.

"I suppose so."

"Can we go ashore here?" Frey asked. "Is there a suitable landing place?"

"Sure, anywhere you like. We can just push ourselves in through the reeds."

"Let's do it," Frey said. "Then we can go for a walk."

A few minutes later we climbed ashore and secured the *kano*'s painter to a bunch of reeds. Frey marched off along the barge path, which was slightly elevated on a low dike surrounding the fields. I grabbed her hand, half running, half hopping along, trying to keep up with her long strides. We stopped at the next bend of the canal where we could see the greenhouses and vegetable fields in the distance. To our right was a large expanse of empty meadow, as far as the eye could see. Close behind us was the edge of the forest. Next to us, at our feet, was the calm water of the canal with its reeds and lilies and the ducks going about their business. Except for us and the ducks, there wasn't a living soul in sight.

We were about to sit down to enjoy our tranquil surroundings when suddenly the peace and quiet turned into chaos. Planes came roaring over, seeming to have come out of nowhere. Above the forest they dove, dropping bombs: explosions! *Rat-ta-ta-ta*, machine-gun fire burst from the wings of the planes. We could see the British insignia on their hulls. They were aiming at whatever the Germans were building or hiding in the forest. Then German fighter planes were in the air and in pursuit of the attackers. One plane was hit and came roaring down with a high-pitched scream, spewing smoke from its tail. It crashed and hit the ground just a short distance away from us. Frey pulled me off the dike and we ducked into a little hollow where we huddled close together, heads down, our hands clasped behind our necks. Soon it was over. The fallen plane was on fire, the others disappearing into the distance. "Let's get out of here," Frey yelled, pulling me up. We ran to the place where the *kano* was tied up. Just as we jumped in, another explosion echoed past our ears. It was the crashed plane. Bits of metal and earth rained down around us. We took to the paddles and forced the water past the hull. The *kano* sliced through the water, taking us home.

We got away unscathed, but this little adventure made us

realize that it wasn't only the Germans we had to watch out for. We were also under attack from our friends, the British. It became common to hear fighter planes flying overhead. We never knew where the bombs might fall, but for a while, at least, our neighbourhood escaped destruction.

Another time my family went out for a weekend trip in our sailboat. To my delight, Frey had joined us. We were nearing Rijnsaterwoude, a small village by the lake. As we came closer to the shore, we spotted soldiers, trucks, and what looked to be general confusion in the village.

"It's a *razzia* (raid)," Pa whispered. "Too late to turn back; they've already spotted us."

Sure enough, two German officers were pointing at us, one with a pair of binoculars trained on us. As we came closer, we could see the smiles on their faces. They had seen my father and brother, obvious candidates for transport to Germany. They hailed us and indicated a place at the quay where they wanted us to dock. They called to a group of soldiers who promptly marched to the spot. They took our mooring lines and secured the boat. We were told to disembark, and the two officers, hands folded behind their backs, walked around us, examining their prey. Then they ordered me, my mother, and Frey to go back on board. My father and brother were escorted to a building. All this time my brother was talking to one of the officers, showing him his fake papers. Before they reached the building I saw the officer saluting my brother, who then turned and sauntered back to our boat. My father was taken inside.

"What about your father?" my mother said as Folkert stepped aboard. It was amazing: my brother with his flair and fake papers was treated like an important person, while my father, legitimately exempt from labour in Germany because of his job with the police force, was arrested.

"I don't know; there must be some question about his papers. Don't worry. We'll give it a few minutes and if it's not sorted out by then, I'll go and get him."

"You'll get him? How?"

"Leave it to me; I know how to deal with those characters. You just have to bluff your way through."

"No, no," said Mam and Frey. "They'll keep you too."

"Not a chance. Really, don't worry, I'll get him out."

We waited ten minutes. Pa was still inside.

"Okay, that's long enough," my brother said, and before we could interfere he jumped off the boat. Confidently he walked to the building. We could see him flashing his papers to the guard who stood by the door and then he went in. After what seemed like eternity, but was in fact only about ten minutes, he came out again, accompanied by my father. We breathed a sigh of relief.

7

One of our guests who stayed with us for a whole week was a
fun guy. I guess he was Jewish because when he arrived late at
night he wore one of those yellow armbands with a star on it over
his jacket. As soon as he stepped into the house he ripped it off,
threw it into the fireplace, and burned it. His wife had one too.
It also went into the fireplace. Apparently he was in the furniture
business because he started to tell us all about the chairs, tables,
and cabinets that were in our home. To me he pointed out a carving that was in the centre of the doors of the tea chest in the living
room.

"Do you know what that is for?" he asked.

I shook my head and shrugged my shoulders.

"Well, I'll tell you. Do you have a dart game? Do you have any
darts?"

"Yes," I answered.

"Okay, then, in the centre of this carving there is a little knob.
See it?"

I took a close look and told him that I could see it.

"Well, that is where you aim your darts. If you hit that little
knob you get the highest score."

I looked at him doubtfully. "Really?"

"Stop it, Sam; don't put crazy ideas into the boy's head," said
Sam's wife disapprovingly. "Don't listen to him," she added, looking at me. "He's just kidding."

"Yeah, just kidding," Sam said, giving me a wink. "Better not damage your mother's nice furniture. Do you play checkers?"

"Yes, sir," I answered.

"Okay, then, get the board and the pieces, and let's play."

From then on, every day, we played several games while his wife chatted with my mother. When they left, Sam said, "We are going to Switzerland. I'll be back soon, when the war is over, and then we can play some more games. You take care of yourself, okay?" I shook his hand and felt sad.

A little while after this I overheard a discussion between my father and Folkert about "the operation." I was playing on the floor of the dining room with my Meccano set. You could build a lot of interesting things with Meccano, using all the metal parts that you connected with the bolts, nuts, and washers it came with. I was making a crane that could load cargo onto one of my toy trucks. Mam, Pa, and Folkert were sitting at the table. Mam was reading and my father and Folkert were talking. I usually wasn't all that interested in grown-up talk, but this time, for no particular reason, and although still concentrating on my building project, I perked up my ears. Perhaps it was the talk about foreign countries and names of faraway cities and other places that caught my interest. I gathered that while my father and brother had been tidying up the *schuur* earlier in the day, they had been approached by a man who said he had something urgent to discuss with my father. He had said that he wanted to meet with him later that night at an address a few blocks away from our place.

"What do you think he wants?" asked my brother.

"I know what he wants. They're having a meeting tonight and probably want to talk me into joining their organization, the Resistance. He's a member of the police force and we've known each other for a long time. He mentioned it once before."

"Are you thinking of joining? Do they know about our operation?" asked Folkert.

"No! They don't know, and I'm not going to join."

"Why not?" Folkert asked. "It seems to me that the bigger the organization is, the more power it will have. Also, what about expenses? Often we don't have enough ration tickets and we end up having to buy food on the black market. That's expensive and I'm certain there are other costs. What about those guys at the borders, for instance? And the cost of transportation and whatever else? Wouldn't it help if we had more people to support the operation?"

"Not in this case. So far, cost hasn't been a problem. It is explained to the people we help. Those who have no money are supported by those who have; the affluent ones are charged, and the others are not. We have ways of checking out their financial situation, and I must say that those with money have been very supportive and have not complained. If we become entangled with the Resistance, more people get involved, and that I want to avoid. In our case, more people means more vulnerability. We're better off keeping it as small and tight as possible. I know everyone in the chain intimately. The guys at the borders I have known for years; they are experienced operators and I trust them. For all I know, any Tom, Dick, or Harry can join the Resistance. No doubt, many of them are sincere, trustworthy, and capable men, but some are just loudmouths who brag a lot but have little or nothing worthwhile to offer. When the chips are down they'll foul up and jeopardize everyone connected with them. We don't need them and I don't want to risk our entire operation because some nitwit does something stupid for the sake of impressing his friends.

"At present we have one man in Limburg, one in Belgium, one in France, and one in Switzerland. The fellow in Limburg knows the Belgian, but he does not know the man in France; the man in France only knows the Belgian and the Swiss. The Swiss fellow only knows the Frenchman. I know all of them, so besides me, only the people who are transported and therefore meet every contact will know everyone involved. They won't betray us because they have too much at stake themselves—unless they're caught. But that's the risk we'll have to take. In addition, there are the other people who operate safe houses, but they don't know each other, nor do they know any of those involved in the chain."

"What about little brother here? He knows quite a bit too."

I looked up when I heard that.

"Yes," Pa said, "but he's part of the operation, and he won't tell anybody, will you, Jan?"

"No, Vader, of course not!"

"That's my boy." He got up from the table, looked at my almost finished crane, and ruffled my hair. Then he looked at his watch and said, "Well, it's about that time. I'd better go and tell him no. I'll be back soon." He picked up his hat and walked out the door.

Now I had a better grasp of what was going on. Pa had organized a chain that allowed people fleeing from the Germans to escape to Switzerland, which was neutral.

As time went on we had people staying at the house more frequently. Sometimes they stayed for just a few days, sometimes several weeks. One day Pa took me with him when he went to see some other people. We called at eleven different addresses where I was introduced to the people who lived there. Then a few weeks later we went there again. Afterwards, Pa asked me if I would be able to find my way back to all these places. I figured I could, and he said, "Okay, we'll see if you're right." The next day we went again. This time I led the way. We didn't stop at any of the doors; as soon as we arrived at one, Pa said, "That's good. Now, where is the next one?" Eventually, when we had passed each address, he said, "You've passed the test, you found them all. Next time you will have to go on your own, call at each one of them, and deliver a message from me. Just say, "Vader asked me to say hello.""

I looked at him, puzzled. "Vader asked me to say hello?"

"Yes, that's all you have to say." He hesitated, and then explained, "It's a coded message, which they will understand. It's safer for you to deliver it than me, because no one will suspect a little boy. If I or your brother or even Mam does this, it will arouse more suspicion."

After that, every once in a while I wound my way through the streets, usually on my roller skates, calling at the various addresses. I soon noticed that often on that same day, sometimes the next, any guests staying at our house would leave. I guess the addresses were other safe houses, and my message told them to prepare their guests for transport to Switzerland.

One set of guests stayed on and on at our house: Isaac and Lena. After several months they were joined by Jaap, Lena's brother. I liked Jaap—he was a nice guy—and Isaac was not too bad either, but Lena was a quarrelsome woman. She had dyed red hair, a big nose, and big lips with lots of red lipstick. She was large, shorter than but twice as wide as my mother, who was a tall and slender woman. When Lena first arrived she pretended to be nice and made quite a fuss about me, but I didn't like her and I knew that she didn't like me either. My mother told me not to judge her. "She is a worried lady," Mam said, "and misses her daughter who is staying with other people." I thought she was jealous because I lived with my parents in relative freedom while her daughter did not. Many times she made snide remarks to me, something like "You don't know how lucky you are. You can just hang around and play with your friends while my daughter is locked up in a house with strange people." This was not quite true. Her daughter was staying with very nice people and often they brought her over to visit.

With our three guests staying long-term at the house, my brother spent a lot of time on the boat. It had been moved to a small marina near the Kaag, a lake not far from the city of Leiden. The marina was owned by a farmer, and several of the boats moored there were also occupied by young men who were hiding from the Germans. The farmer fed them in return for their help with running the farm.

I liked the new place because it was a lot closer to home, which meant that every now and then I could go and stay with my brother for a few days. Sometimes I went there in the tram and sometimes in my *kano*. It was a long paddle, about fifteen kilometres; but most of the time, when Frey went with me, we hitched a ride with one of the motorized barges. Most of the bargemen objected to towing us along, but sometimes we found one who was friendly and didn't mind doing it. It was kind of scary because the barges were fast and the speed lifted the bow of the *kano* right out of the water. Sometimes we got invited aboard. Then Frey chatted with the bargeman's wife in the barge's cozy living quarters and I got to stay at the wheel with the bargeman. Some would let me steer, and it got especially exciting when, after they had watched for a while and saw that I was doing a good job, they'd leave me alone at the wheel while they tended to a quick chore on deck.

It was neat to watch the goings-on on board the barges. It was a completely different way of life. When the bargeman's wife needed groceries, she would raise a flag and soon a *parlevinker* would come alongside. *Parlevinkers* were small, fast boats that were like floating grocery stores. When a *parlevinker* skipper saw a flag, he would chase the barge and tie up alongside. Then the skipper's wife hopped over, did her shopping, and came back on board with the groceries. The barge never stopped while this was going on, so there was no time lost. When the shopping was done, the *parlevinker* skipper detached his boat and went on his merry way, looking for other customers. Of course, with the food and fuel shortages, the *parlevinkers* were not as plentiful, nor did they carry as many supplies, although they and the barge operators appeared to fare better than the stores and people of the big cities.

I think it was during one of these barge trips that I decided that I was going to become a sea captain when I was older, just like my grandfather and great-grandfather. I loved listening to my grandfather's stories about faraway places, about adventures at sea and different ports. He was born at sea, aboard the ship on which my great-grandfather and great-grandmother lived and worked. Opa had met his wife, my grandmother, because of his job. There was a certain drawbridge through which my grandfather's ship had to travel when coming into home port. Fees had to be paid at drawbridges. As the bridge was raised and the ship went through, the bridge-keeper in his high perch would lower a small wooden shoe, attached to a rod with a string, into which the skipper would deposit the fee. At this particular bridge the collecting was usually done by the bridge-keeper's daughter. Every time my grandfather came through, in addition to the fee, written notes went up and down in the shoe. Eventually, that bridge-keeper's daughter became my grandmother.

I loved to hear this story; I asked for it every time I visited my grandparents. I was curious about what was written in the notes, but when I asked Opa, he always answered, "Well, maybe sometime when you're grown up, I'll tell you." Oma didn't want to go to sea and that's how Opa became a landlubber and started a small shipyard.

One weekend, when Frey couldn't come along to visit my brother, my friend Wim came with me instead. Pa put us on the tram to Leiden. When we arrived in Leiden, we started the long walk to the farm where the boat was moored. Just outside the city we got lucky, because we managed to hitch a ride with a farmer on his way home from the market. We rode in a horse-drawn wagon. The farmer seemed pleased with the company and was chatting away happily about his day at the market. As it turned out his farm was close to the one we were aiming for. The route was along the Zijl, a river that flowed into the Kaag, and as the horse plodded along, we enjoyed watching the traffic of barges and other boats on the river. Wim was very excited because he had never been here before. He was especially looking forward to spending a weekend on the boat, another adventure he had never experienced.

When we arrived at the boat, my brother introduced us to

A typical Dutch haystack (sketch by the author).

some of his pals, four other guys about his age, all of them hiding from the Germans. We felt pretty important being included among this elite group, each one of them being at least twice our age. That evening my brother cooked supper: slices of bread fried in butter and covered with young Gouda cheese made on the farm. It was delicious! We hadn't had a meal like that as far back as we could remember. That night we slept on the boat, curled up in our cozy bunks.

The next day, my brother showed us around the farm. There was the courtyard, a horseshoe-shaped area paved with cobblestones, the open end flanked by the canal in which the boats were moored. On the one side, there was a big barn with farm equipment and stalls for the horses; the farmhouse was in the middle with a cow barn behind, and a large haystack was on the other side. It was a typical Dutch haystack, with a roof mounted on four poles. The roof could slide up and down the poles with the help of a winch and cable. As the pile of hay got smaller, the roof was lowered to keep the hay dry.

To allow the roof to slide up and down easily, the poles were greased. There is a saying about the near impossibility of finding a needle in a haystack; just as unlikely was climbing the poles, especially when there was hay stacked inside. The hay pressed against the inside of the poles, making it impossible to get your arms and legs around them.

Beside the haystack, the fellows staying on the boats had erected a pole with a basketball net. As we were being shown around the farm, a game was in progress. We had stopped to watch when suddenly one of the players yelled, "I hear a speed-boat!"

Instantly the game stopped. Everyone strained their ears to listen. Sure enough, the sound grew louder as the engine noise of a fast boat came closer. It was another *razzia*: the Germans were scouting the area for hiding men. "Run for it, guys!" one of the fellows shouted. "They're heading this way!"

The guys scattered in every direction, each running for some hiding place—except one. He just stood there, frozen, not know-ing where to go or what to do. "Run, run," both Wim and I shouted. "Get away from here! The Nazis are coming."

Bewildered, the fellow looked around him. He stepped this way and that way, then looked at the haystack that was filled to the top. He ran toward it looking for a ladder. There wasn't one. So he grabbed one of the poles and went up. He didn't climb—he more or less ran up the pole, like a monkey.

Wim and I stared open-mouthed as the fellow reached the top and disappeared into the hay. Fortunately, the speedboat passed by and its passengers didn't even look in our direction. If it had been the Germans, I'm certain our astonished faces would have been a dead giveaway.

We were still staring at the haystack when the others, after realizing that it had been a false alarm, returned one by one to the courtyard. "What's the matter?" my brother said. "Did you see a ghost?"

We both pointed to the haystack. "He...he...climbed up the pole."

"What do you mean, he climbed up the pole?"

The others had now gathered around us.

"Honestly, he climbed up; he just sort of...*ran* up the pole. He's in the haystack."

"Who's in the haystack?" They now looked around, taking stock of themselves. "Who is missing? Fred, where is Fred?"

"He's in the haystack, honestly. He went up one of the poles. Didn't he, Wim?"

"Yes," said Wim. "I saw it too."

Now everybody was looking up at the haystack.

"Impossible," one of them said.

"Fred," another one yelled, "are you up there?"

Some movement could be heard from way up high. Then a head peered over the edge. "Have they left? Are they gone?"

"Yes, you can come down now."

Nervously, Fred looked down from his perch, only his head showing. "I can't. I'm scared of heights."

It took a ladder and a lot of prompting to get Fred moving. Finally, with the help of two more ladders and the combined efforts of his buddies, Fred was down on solid ground.

Later that day, he was offered anything under the sun to give a demonstration and repeat his performance. But nothing could persuade him to do it again.

It reminded me of the time when Dick and I were being chased by the German soldiers. We didn't really jump across that irrigation ditch; we flew, propelled by adrenalin. It's amazing what people are capable of when in fear for their lives!

8

One day Pa brought home a present: a dog! He had wiry, brownish fur and one ear that stood straight up and one that was floppy. We became best friends instantly. On Folkert's suggestion, I named him Spunky. Spunky went with me in the *kano*, chased after me when I roller skated, and came along when I delivered messages to the other safe houses.

In late 1943, when I was eleven, Isaac, Lena, and Jaap had been with us for almost a year. They didn't want to go to Switzerland because they wanted to stay close to their daughter, who was living with another family not too far from our home. The situation was becoming risky; Lena insisted on seeing her daughter at the most inopportune moments. Most times we could arrange to have her daughter brought to our house, but sometimes Lena insisted on paying her a sudden visit. She imagined that the girl was not being treated right, though nothing was further from the truth— the people she was staying with adored the little girl and treated her as their own child. Yet there was no reasoning with Lena. In the middle of the day she would demand to go out and see her daughter. Then she ranted and raved when my mother and father tried to explain to her why that was impossible. Her husband, Isaac, also tried to make her listen to reason. "It's too dangerous, darling; you can't go outside on the street. That's why we're here in this house. We are hiding from the Germans. If they catch you, we'll all be in danger and they might catch our little Betsy too."

My mother was afraid that someday Lena would just go before we could stop her. It all came to a head one day when Lena took her frustration out on me.

We often passed the time by playing board games, and sometimes Jaap and I arm-wrestled or did push-ups while Spunky jumped around us. One day, when I was on the floor doing push-ups with Jaap, Lena grabbed me by my ankles, lifted me up, and then, when I was hanging upside down, just let go, dropping me on my head. Jaap got very angry with her. Mam came in from the kitchen when she heard the noise and wanted to know what had happened. Lena said it was an accident, but I knew she had done it on purpose. I don't think Mam believed her either because that evening I heard her talking to my father about it.

"She is a vindictive and unreasonable woman, always criticizing, always complaining. She thinks everyone is against her," Mam said. "I know she's caught in a nasty situation, but we all are and we have to make the best of it. There's no excuse for her to act the way she does. She's going to get us all into trouble—I know it. It's time they move on. Lena should be happy: little Betsy is safe. Everyone thinks she's the daughter of the couple she's staying with. Nobody, except us and her immediate family, knows that the child is Jewish."

Not long after that, Jaap, Isaac, and Lena were evacuated to Switzerland. Our house was back to normal again. But it didn't last long. In November, about three weeks after the guests left, Mam and Pa and I were sitting in the kitchen. Spunky was lying by my feet. It was about ten o'clock in the morning and we were alone; we had no other people staying with us.

The doorbell rang and Spunky jumped up and barked. Pa asked me to go to the door to see who it was. When I opened the door, two men stepped inside and pushed past me into the house. Two others remained outside. The two who had entered walked through the vestibule into the hallway. At the end of the hallway was the kitchen; the door was open and they could see my mother and father. They walked in and told my father to come with them. They accused him of being a traitor; he was being arrested. One of the men spoke German, the other one was Dutch. The German appeared to be in charge. My mother got up from her seat, but the German pulled out a pistol and told her to remain seated. "Pack some clothes and toiletries for him," said the Dutch fellow to my mother. Mam hurried to the closet for a small suitcase and filled it with the required items. In the meantime, the two men who had been outside had also come into the house. "Search the place," the German said to them. "Find the Jews." While they were searching, my father was marched out the door.

Pa turned around. "Don't worry," he said to us, "I'll get this sorted out and I'll be back soon." I followed as they descended the stairs of the portico. "Vader," I yelled, "where are you going?" By now they were on the street. "I'll be back soon," Pa shouted again, but one of the men told him to be quiet.

The other men, who had completed their search and had come up empty-handed, pushed past me, joining the others. Mam was standing by the door; she called me and handed me the suitcase. "Quick," she said. "Go, give this to Pa."

With the suitcase I ran back down the stairs. I saw the men, with my father, walking on the street. I ran after them and when I caught up, I handed the suitcase to Pa. "Thanks, Jan," Pa said as he grabbed the suitcase from me. "I'll be back soon!" The men wouldn't let him stop for a moment. They grabbed his arms and pulled him along. I was still following, trying to keep up with their fast pace, Spunky bouncing close beside me. Suddenly, the Dutch fellow turned around. "You go back to your mother, and stay there." Spunky growled, but I grabbed him and held him back.

Keeping some distance, we kept following, but then they climbed into the tram at the tram stop, a few blocks away from our home. I stood there and watched helplessly as it drove away. I saw the streetcar speed down a long road; soon it was out of sight.

With a big lump in my throat, I turned around and Spunky and I reluctantly went back to the apartment. When we got inside, Mam was sitting in the kitchen, crying. I cried too. Spunky jumped up against me and licked my face and hands.

The next day, a letter was delivered to my mother, pushed under the front door. It had no return address and no signature.

Isaac became ill and had to be left behind in France. Just learned that he has been arrested. The others, including Lena, reached destination and are safe. Lena blames us. She has contacted the Nazis and offered information in exchange for release of her husband. All operatives notified.

The letter had come too late to save my father.

9

A few days later, on November 10, 1943, we received another letter, this one from the state commissioner of occupied Netherlands' territory. It informed us that my father had been released from his duties as an officer of the Dutch police force.

"So much for that," Mam said. "But I'm more concerned with his return. When will he be back here with us?"

We still had high hopes that he would suddenly walk through the door—until we received a message from someone in the police force. Apparently, he had originally been detained in the prison in Scheveningen and had since been moved to Vught. Then we knew his return was not likely to happen in the near future. Vught was a concentration camp in Holland with a terrible reputation. We were very, very worried.

Weeks…months…half a year went by, with not a word from Pa. We sent him letters and packages with food and cookies Mam had baked, hoping he would receive them. Whether he did or not, we did not know until April 1944, when we finally received a letter from him. It came from Vught and bore a stamp of approval from a German censor.

Dear Wife and Boys,

As I start I don't know what to write, yet I have so much to tell. But, fortunately, I am doing all right and hope that this is also the case with you. This week I am very depressed. The longing

Der Reichskommissar
für die besetzten niederländischen Gebiete.

Auf Grund des $ 1 der Verordnung über die Ausübung der
Regierungsbefugnisse in den Niederlanden vom 29 Mai 1940 und unter
Bezug auf das ''Allgemeine Beamtenrecht'' entlasse ich den Oberwacht-
meister der niederländischen Polizei

Folkert de G r o o t ,
Den Haag, mit sofortiger Wirkung aus dem Dienst der niederländischen
Polizei.

Den Haag, den 10. November 1943.

In Vertretung:
Der Genralkommissar für das Sicherheitswesen:
w.g. Rauter.
S.S. Obergruppenführer und General der Polizei.

Voor eensluidend afschrift,
Chef Bureau Pensioenen, Afdeeling Politie,
Ministerie van Justitie,

G.B. Mersch.

Letter from German command stating that my father had been relieved
of his duties in the police force.

for you is so strong that often I feel very discouraged, as if it will never end. I do not believe that I will see you soon. It will probably be at least another six months before I can be with you again. I had also hoped to receive a letter from you this week, but nothing has arrived. You do write to me, don't you? I have received the parcel. You baked some delicious cookies, Moekie [my mother's nickname]. When shall I be able to do that again? How are things with the garden, have you seeded? And Jan, does he do his best in school? Remember, Jan, you promised to work hard. Do your best, Jan, to graduate to the next grade. Folkert, are you okay too? Jan must have grown. Every time I see myself getting on that tram, I can see him running after me with that little suitcase. How is it, Moekie; are you certain you can afford to send me those cookies and bread? Otherwise, don't send it. I have enough to eat here. Only maybe a little bit of butter, or jam, or syrup. That, I really have a craving for. I have no shortage of food here and I know very well that you need it badly. So, don't send me any more food. You asked me in your last letter about vitamins. Yes, those are finished. But don't send any, they are too scarce and difficult to get and I don't see the advantage of having them here anyway. Now, Moekie and boys, many kisses from me. Your husband and father.

We were very excited to receive his letter and we read it over and over again. But each time we also felt sad.

The next letter was dated May 21. This time, on the back there was a notation that said Nr. 8245, Block 15. I guess that was his number and location in the camp.

Dear Moekie and Boys,

It is still the same. I am doing well and I hope you are too. With longing I think of you and home and a letter from you. I'm glad to hear the garden is doing well. Yes, you need lots of water right now, especially in the planters. It is highly necessary that I come home. It is impossible for you to keep up with all that. Jan is graduating, I hear—congratulations, Jan. That makes me happy, my boy; that is good for yourself and great for Moekie and Vader. I would really like to be able to chat with you all. If only they would give me a few days, then I could fix the garden and spend some time with you. Oh well, let's hope that there will soon be an end to this terrible war. People hate each other and they don't even know why. With Frey and Folkert everything goes well, eh? Every time I hear about the bombing I think of you with fright. In The Hague there must have been a lot of changes because of the bombs. Yes, Moekie—what else do I need to write? Oh, yes, I have received your parcel, but the fish was not in it. You couldn't get any, I assume. Oh well, with the smallest morsels I am happy, because it means I have heard from you again. There is a lot to talk about and much I would like to hear from you, but there is not enough space on this little piece of paper. Therefore, Moekie, I'll finish with many kisses for you and the boys. Give my greetings to all our friends and please, think of me. Folkert, you are helping your mother right? And Jan, do your best. Goodbye Moekie, many kisses, bye!

The garden that Pa mentioned in his letter was a piece of land on the outskirts of the city. Pa had built a one-room cabin on it. The name was painted in big letters on the front: De Blok Hut (The Block Cabin). Inside the cabin was a small stove and a counter with a sink with running water. The only furniture was a table and chairs. Sometimes we stayed there overnight, curled up on the floor in sleeping bags. Next to the cabin Pa had built a storage shed for the garden equipment. In the front, outside, there was a small patio with lounge chairs and a table with a large parasol.

I liked gardening with Pa, turning the soil with a spade and working manure into it, then planting and weeding and watching the plants grow. A large section was planted with flowers. These were for Mam and every time we were at the garden, we would cut some and take them home. Folkert wasn't into gardening, but

Spunky loved coming with us. He'd chase butterflies or gnaw on a bone that he had buried somewhere. We had to keep a close eye on him, because we didn't want him to damage the plants. Pa grew lots of vegetables: beans, lettuce, carrots, and potatoes. I especially liked the beans because they climbed up against sticks we put into the ground and they had pretty flowers.

We lost interest in the garden when Pa was taken away, but after receiving his first letter, the whole family pitched in to sort the place out. Even Frey joined the work party.

Sometime after we received the second letter, Dick, Tonny, and I went for a wander, exploring the neighbourhood and eventually ending up in the vicinity of the forest Overvoorde. Spunky was with us, galloping around and sniffing at various interesting objects. From time to time he would run off to chase a bird or whatever else aroused his interest. We discovered a small mound crowded with ants. We hunched down to examine it, using a twig to carefully touch and poke into the little hill, into which the ants were busy carrying small objects from various locations. Suddenly I realized that Spunky had been gone longer than usual.

I stood up and looked around. "Where is Spunky?" I said to Dick and Tonny. They also stood up and scanned the area. We called but he did not come. We walked and called, searching the area. No Spunky. Eventually it started getting dark and we had to go home. I hoped that maybe Spunky had gone home too. But when we arrived there was no sign of him.

Several days went by. We went back to the vicinity of the ant-hill, still searching for Spunky. I made signs and posted them on lampposts, street signs, doors of stores, walls of buildings, but Spunky remained missing. I was very, very sad.

Folkert helped, bringing home a puppy one day. It was a female chow chow. She had thick reddish fur and a blue tongue. She looked just like a cuddly little bear, so I named her Beertje (Little Bear). She was a smart little dog and it didn't take very long to housetrain her.

Beertje was more of a house dog than Spunky and, except for regular walks, did not really play with me and my friends. So I still missed Spunky somewhat. I knew, though, that he would not be coming back. During the time I had searched for him, I had overheard Folkert saying to my mother, "I bet someone caught him and butchered him for food." I did not want to believe it but deep down I knew that was probably what had happened, because people had become pretty desperate. Food was scarcer than ever. Some kids had *honger oedeem*—big bellies, swollen by starvation.

Pa's next letters were dated June 4 and June 18, 1944. The contents were much the same, but we noticed that my father's handwriting, which was normally very elegant and stylish, was slowly deteriorating. The letters were becoming more difficult to read. Was he starving, too, in the prison camp?

Mam decided to continue my piano lessons, now that we no longer had people staying with us. We hardly recognized Mr. Geenjaar when he arrived, he was suffering so from malnutrition. He had become much thinner and looked fragile. He brought a carrot for lunch which he carefully unwrapped, sliced into little pieces and chewed while he listened to me playing the exercises.

One day, when Mam and I went to the garden, we got a shock. It had been totally devastated. The carrots and lettuce had disappeared, the potatoes had been dug up, and even the beans, although not yet ready for picking, were torn from the plants. We stared at the depressing scene. Obviously, people had plundered anything that was even remotely edible.

"I have been expecting this for some time," Mam said. "It was only a matter of time until people discovered what was growing here." With a sigh she grabbed my hand and said, "We'd better not tell Pa about this; it'll break his heart. Come, let's go back home. There's nothing more we can do here." But we wandered through the garden one more time. It was pretty sad. So much hard work had been put into this. However, when people are hungry, they become desperate. We couldn't really blame them.

At my desk in grade five (1943), Winterweg school, The Hague.

Not only food but also clothing was scarce. I had outgrown my shoes; many kids were dressed in rags. Months before the end of the school year in 1944, many schools were already closed. Wood for paper and pencils was scarce; the rubber that erasers are made of was needed by the Germans for tires for their vehicles. (Anything made of copper was also seized by the Germans; it was needed for shell casings.)

My school had stayed open and did better than any of the others, mainly because of Mr. Boon and our puppet theatre. Over the couple of years I had Mr. Boon as a teacher, we had turned that class project into a lifesaver. Mr. Boon made deals with other schools where our class performed in exchange for writing paper, books, pencils, and erasers. We played all over the city as well:

for the mayor and his councillors, for the press and radio. We played for the employees of large bakeries where we were paid with loaves of bread, and for a dairy outfit in exchange for milk.

This was my last year in elementary school, and Mam had already enrolled me in the MULO, a sort of high school, for the fall. A celebration was to be held at the school for the graduating class, and all the students and their parents were invited. Mr. Boon decided that we should perform one more puppet play to celebrate the occasion. This time, we would do the musical that Wim and I had written. I was to play the piano, while the other kids performed with the puppets. The school rented a nice grand piano for the purpose. It was positioned on the stage next to and a little bit in front of the puppet theatre. I was nervous about this, since a lot of the attention now centred on me. Just before we started, Mr. Boon took me aside. "Look, Jan, you have done this many times before. A much larger audience makes no difference. As soon as the curtain opens, don't pay attention to all those people. Just play that piano and concentrate on the play. Think of the puppet theatre, of the puppets, of the story; stay in your own world and separate yourself from what's going on with the audience. Just keep your eyes on the keyboard and the puppet stage. Don't worry about a thing, because I know you can do it."

I sat down at the piano and the curtains opened. With awe I looked at the mass of people in the audience; then I remembered what Mr. Boon had said and watched the puppet theatre. Its curtains opened, I started to play, and the first puppet appeared and began to sing. My nerves settled down, and soon I was lost in the play. The reactions of the audience were familiar, boosting adrenalin and encouraging our concentration.

When the play was over, people stood up, applauding. The puppeteers lined up in front of the puppet theatre, and Mr. Boon came on stage and pulled me over to them. Again, tremendous applause. We bowed; the curtains closed and then reopened. Again we bowed. It had been an exhilarating experience.

Pa said something about it in his next letter, dated July 2, 1944. "Great that you already are a pianist, Jan, and performed at that farewell party at school. That was fun, eh? Now you see that it is fun to be able to play the piano. Keep studying, boy!"

We noticed that the block number had changed from 15 to 16. He had been moved to a different location in the camp. This time, the handwriting was better and easier to read. The instructions printed on the paper in German said "*Nur die Zeilen beschreiben*" ("Write only on the lines") but there was more space to write now, four pages instead of one, although the line spaces were wider.

In his letter, Pa also said that he was proud that I had graduated and encouraged me to keep on studying so that when I became a sea captain, he and my mother could go on a journey with me to Indonesia and to America.

In his previous letters Pa had said something about a mysterious package that he received from an unknown person. It was again mentioned in a letter that came on July 17, 1944, a short one on a small piece of paper.

Dear Wife and children. Everything is well and also with you I hope. I expected to get a letter from you this week, but haven't received anything. I did receive your package but please don't send any more because every week I get a terrific parcel, with ½ lb of butter, a jar of jam, cheese, cookies, sausage. A nice package that you can't afford to send. If you send me packages as well, I get nothing. How is it at home, Moekie, can you get vegetables and potatoes? It's taking a long time. What an ordeal, I have difficulties coping with it. Often I lie awake during the entire night—always thinking of you and the boys. I know, that doesn't help any, but what can I do about it? Why they're keeping us here for such a long time, I don't know. Have they just forgotten about us? On what are they actually basing the difference in punishment? One person gets half a year, and for others there is no end in sight. I would have liked so much to be home for Jan's birthday,

never mind my own birthday, but I don't expect that will be hap-
pening. There is no progress, one can't understand why it is taking
so long. Well, Moekie and boys, chin up. Many greetings, kisses
from me. Pa, bye!

It was a relief to know that Pa was getting regular food par-
cels. We were coping to a certain extent because Folkert was still
changing the ration tickets to our benefit. But even with the tickets, we were not guaranteed food. People pushed and shoved one
another in the long lineups at the bakeries, hoping that when their
turn finally came, the bread would not be sold out. The same happened at the greengrocers'.

There was other food available, hidden from officials and sold
on the so-called black market. Here, opportunists made a lot
of money by selling items at high prices: a loaf of bread for as
much as 125 guilders—a monthly wage for many people; a sack of
wheat for 500 guilders. Many people from the city travelled long
distances, by foot or on a bicycle—on bare rims, for if the Germans hadn't taken them, the tires had worn out and couldn't be
replaced—to barter directly with farmers. They took along their
prized possessions, such as fur coats and jewellery, to trade them
for wheat, potatoes, vegetables, or anything else that could be
eaten.

Once we heard about a lady who unravelled part of a bedcover. She knitted the salvaged wool into socks, which she took
to a farmer and traded for food. As she was about to leave, the
farmer's wife said, "If you have more socks, come back, I'll take
them." So the lady kept unravelling more of the bedcover and
knitting more socks. One day, the sock-knitting lady said to the
farmer's wife, "If you don't mind my asking, what in the world
do you do with so many socks?" "Well," said the farmer's wife, "I
unravel them; I'm knitting a bedcover."

Everything was scarce. Electricity was on for only a few hours
a day. There was no gas for cooking, and no coal—my mother's

Der Tag der Entlassung kann jetzt noch nicht angegeben
werden. Besuche im Lager sind verboten. Anfragen
sind zwecklos.

Auszug aus der Lagerordnung:

Jeder Häftling darf im Monat 2 Briefe oder Postkarten empfangen und absenden. Eingehende Briefe dürfen nicht mehr als 4 Seiten à 15 Zeilen enthalten und müssen übersichtlich und gut lesbar sein. Geldsendungen sind nur durch Postanweisung zulässig, deren Abschnitt nur Vor-, Zuname, Geburtstag, Häftlingsnummer trägt, jedoch keinerlei Mitteilungen. Geld, Fotos und Bildereinlagen in Briefen sind verboten. Die Annahme von Postsendungen, die den gestellten Anforderungen nicht entsprechen, wird verweigert. Unübersichtliche, schlecht lesbare Briefe werden vernichtet. Im Lager kann alles gekauft werden. Nationalsozialistische Zeitungen sind zugelassen, müssen aber vom Häftling selbst im Konzentrationslager bestellt werden. Lebensmittelpakete dürfen zu jeder Zeit und in jeder Menge empfangen werden.

Der Lagerkommandant

Lieve Vrouw en kinderen alles goed ors thuis hoop ik. Ik had
dier week nog een brief verwacht van jullie. Doch het was niet. Je pakket
heb ik ontvangen Kik. Doch stuur nu niet meer ik krijg alle week een
pracht pakket ½ ton poh jam, kaas, bok was. Een mooi pakket dat jullie
niet kunnen missen. En adzij mij ook stuur krijg ik niet. Hoe is het
thuis heb hun zij gewoon krijgen en aardapp. Wat duurt het lang
he. Wat een tijd ik kan er haast niet dien door. Vooral lig
ik hele nachte wakken steeds bij jou en de jongens. Ik weet
wel schrijven niets meer of doch wat kan ik er aan doen
Waarom zij ons hier zo lang niet loslaten. Ik weet het niet zouden
zij getro. dies zach verzetten. Wat er verschil in de straffen eige
lijk. De eene is 3 jaar en de ander gen verurteilt. Ik
had zo graag met Jan op verjaardag thuis geweest. Ook thuis
met mijs verjaardag. Doch ik ma er nu niet an denken. Een
tijd gaar schoon in Je begrijpt niet dat het zo lang duurt. Nu
Kik en jongens hou alle ju troei vele groeten en kussen van mij. Uit HB P en aug

beautiful enamelled stove had become useless. We had purchased a little wood stove that my mother cooked on, but everyone was using wood stoves now, and wood was hard to find. Doors, panelling, trim—anything burnable was being torn from houses, cut up into little pieces and fed into the stoves.

One day, Folkert and his friends Wim Kastelijn and Henk van der Meiden decided to go on a search for wood. Dick and I tagged along behind them. Wim and Henk both worked for the city in a capacity which was considered essential service and they were therefore exempt from deportation. We searched along the perimeters of the forest Overvoorde. We were skirting the barbed-wire barricade surrounding the forest when we came upon a vacant area where the trees had been removed. The only barriers were the barbed wire and a sign warning of land mines: *Landminen! Betreten Verboten*!

Suddenly Folkert spotted a log over one metre long and about thirty centimetres thick. The three big guys looked at the sign and then at the log. Wim and Henk shook their heads. But Folkert said, "We need that wood," and climbed over the fence. He walked straight to the log and heaved it onto his shoulders. We watched breathlessly as he carried it back to us. "That will keep the stove going for a while," he said, as he placed the log in Wim's and Henk's outstretched arms before climbing back to safe territory. We found a few more bits and pieces of wood and then headed home.

It was worth the risk. Food had become a critical priority, and without wood, the stove could not be heated and food could not be prepared. In normal times it's hard to understand, but in those days the certainty of wood and food was more important than the mere possibility of being blown up by a land mine.

OPPOSITE PAGE: Pa's letter of July 17, 1944.

10

On August 6, 1944, another letter arrived in our mail slot. The first thing we noticed was that Pa's block number had changed again, to No. 20. Whether that was a good sign or not, we had no idea.

He commented about the length of the war, that it was in its fifth year and coming to an end, but then speculated that it could well go on for another year. He wondered what chaos we would be in after the war ended. He was pleased to hear that we were doing well. Again, he mentioned his regular receipt of the mysterious package. He also mentioned, in this letter and the next one (dated August 22, 1944, one day before my twelfth birthday), people I had never heard of before and details that didn't make any sense to me. For example, he talked about sending "shoes and money to Gihi." I have no idea who that was and what that meant. I wonder now if this was a message in a code only my mother and brother understood. But there was a message for me there, too, and this one was clear: "Congratulations on Jan's birthday. Jan, when I get home you'll get an extra hug."

These were the last letters we received from my father. The next month, September 1944, word spread that the Allies had invaded Holland. The event was named and remembered as Dolle Dinsdag (Crazy Tuesday), since everything went crazy. People were beside themselves with joy. Dutch flags and flags of the House of Orange were flown from the apartment windows. People were celebrating in the streets. The Germans panicked and started to move their troops out of the city.

It was just a rumour; the Allies were nowhere in sight. But the result was the Germans moved all political prisoners, including my father, to a concentration camp in Germany. Later we learned that Crazy Tuesday had prolonged my father's life. Apparently, he had received the death penalty and was supposed to be executed. However, Crazy Tuesday caused such chaos in the German command that he was mixed in with the other prisoners and transported with them to Germany. We didn't know which one; at that point we lost all contact. No more letters, not even a hint that he was still alive.

September 1944. Moeder and I, with Beertje by my side, are sitting outside on the balcony at the rear of the apartment. Moeder is reading a book and I am cleaning my mouse's cage. Suddenly we hear an ear-shattering, thundering noise. It is a frightening sound. Everything around us shakes. Then we see it: a rocket climbing up and up into the sky, bursts of flame coming from its tail. It climbs higher and higher, then it levels out and passes over us, heading in a southwesterly direction, leaving a trail of smoke behind it. Moeder has stood up, her arms wound around me, holding me tight. "This is too much," she stammers, her body trembling. "This is the end; how can we survive this?"

I don't know what to say. I'm trembling with fright. Twenty minutes later, another one is launched. Again we watch as it climbs and sprouts its ugly tail. This one, too, climbs and climbs—and then suddenly it is quiet. No more sound. The flames disappear, the smoke vanishes, just a wisp still hanging in the sky. We see the rocket level out, then make an arc. The front end is now pointing downwards. It is falling! We lose sight of it as it disappears behind the buildings. There's a moment of ominous silence, and then an enormous explosion. Our windows shatter; falling glass is all around us from the windows of the neighbouring apartments. My mother cries; I cry too. We keep our arms wrapped around each other.

We had just witnessed the first launching of the V2.

11

The rockets V1 and V2 were large projectiles the Germans fired from various locations in the Netherlands. Most of them were directed toward London, but after D-Day (June 6, 1944), when the Allied forces had landed on the shores of Normandy, they were also fired at Antwerp in Belgium and other destinations where the Allies had been able to establish a stronghold.

The rockets caused tremendous devastation. They were the size of an airplane and loaded with explosives that detonated only when the rocket had buried itself deep into the ground. Rocks and stones, earth, everything that surrounded it blew out, the debris adding to the damage. One rocket was capable of destroying an entire city block.

By the time a V2 arrived at its destination, it was travelling at three times the speed of sound. First, there was the whip-crack sound of the blast wave, bouncing off the point of impact; just split seconds after that, the flash of actual impact. This was followed by the chaos of the explosion as debris and earth flew skyward. Oddly, it was only afterward that you could hear the sound of the rocket's passage: first the whine and rush of whistling air, then a deafening roar. After that...silence. Unless you were close to the launch site, as we were, there was no warning: by the time a V2 was heard, it was already too late.

In a way, the V1 was even scarier. It travelled slower and people could hear it coming, causing panic and fright. The rockets were fired off steadily. Each time we heard or saw one, we were petrified. The worst of it was the feeling of helplessness. There was nowhere to run, nowhere to hide. All we could do was watch, listen, wait, and hope for the best.

Somehow, after enduring a few days of this, we learned to live with that feeling. It became a subconscious routine: without apparent awareness we listened for each rocket; paused when the noise suddenly stopped; held our breath, waiting for it to fall and to hear it explode; then breathed again, assured that it had fallen elsewhere, not on our home. Thirty seconds was the danger period. If it broke down within that period, it would definitely fall somewhere on our city and cause major bedlam. If it failed after that, it would end up falling into the sea. If it didn't fail, and went on its way, it would reach its target and cause destruction wherever it landed—England, Belgium, France.

The rockets were launched from many different locations. The launchers were mobile, but they needed a firm base to withstand the impact of the launch. Most were fired from paved streets, usually at intersections. The selected area would be closed off by the Germans, and then a group of Germans in charge of the launch would arrive. Soon thereafter tanker trucks filled with alcohol and liquid oxygen appeared on the scene. This stuff was poured into the huge projectiles, which had been brought to the site on a large truck with a long trailer. The gang would fire a few rockets from that location, then pull up stakes and move elsewhere.

Members of the Resistance reported the firing sites to the Allied forces who, shortly after each launch, sent fighter planes and bombers to attack the area. The Germans soon became aware of the spies among the local population and started stringent measures to eliminate the threat. Anyone who was suspected was either shot on the spot or arrested and sent to a German concentration camp. They got so worried and nervous about spies that even people who had picked up a bit of scrap from a fallen rocket were interrogated and shipped off to Germany, or shot on the spot.

Between the falling of faulty rockets and bomb attacks by Allied planes on the launch sites, whole city blocks were destroyed and many people were maimed or killed. In our neighbourhood there was not one unbroken window in any home. Pieces of plywood, tarps...anything that served the purpose was used to close up the gaping holes.

The V2s were causing great consternation and were a major threat to our safety; meanwhile, we worried constantly about Pa. We had heard so many bad stories about the German concentration camps: Dachau, Buchenwald, Auschwitz, Oranienburg, Ravensbrück...all names associated with horror and terror. We were terrified that we would never see Vader again.

The food situation had become desperate too. During the summer, Dick and Tonny and I had been able to make frequent trips in the *kano* to the Westland where we scavenged for veggies, potatoes, and sugar beets. We had had corn for a while too. Back in the spring of 1943, the soccer fields across the canal had been plowed up and planted with corn to feed the German army. We had watched with interest as the corn plants began to take their shape, grew taller and then matured. As soon as it ripened, we headed over there with burlap bags and stuffed them with cobs of corn. Then, one time, the rustling of the corn plants attracted the attention of the soldiers on guard and they began to fire at us. Fortunately, we were well hidden by the tall plants. We managed to load the full bags into the *kano* and escape to our side of the canal without being injured. But when my mother heard about this episode she forbade us to go there again. And now, with autumn approaching, we found the end of the potatoes and sugar beets as well.

From time to time, in spite of the bad situation, we had to try to enjoy ourselves. We all liked reading, but during the day the boarded-up windows made it difficult; in the evenings the lack of electricity made it almost impossible, as candles were no longer available and it was hard to find another source of light. One day

I suddenly had an idea that would address this problem.

I had always been interested in electrical gadgets. I had learned to make crystal radios, little receivers connected to a headset. One of the wire leads had a sharp pin or needle attached to it with which you had to probe the crystal. Different spots on the crystal produced different radio stations. They weren't very reliable, but if you were lucky and hit the right spot, you might get reasonably good reception. I made three, one for Tonny, one for Dick, and one for me. Each set was built into a matchbox and fun to fiddle around with. I also made up a primitive communication system. We ran wires from my room to Dick's room in the apartment upstairs and Tonny's room next door. Each room had a small light bulb and a gadget that operated like a switch, which got its power via a transformer plugged into a wall socket wired into the household system. The three of us could send Morse-type messages to one another—when there was electricity.

I got my idea for supplying light from watching Frey sew. Frey's family lived only a short distance away from us, in the next apartment block. She had several sisters, one of them married. They all lived in the same apartment and, I guess, especially with her sewing, the situation was a bit crowded. As well, thanks to Folkert's forged ration tickets and my expeditions to the Westland and the cornfields, we had more food. Frey therefore spent most of her days with us, arriving early in the morning and not leaving until late in the evening.

I took the dynamo and the headlamp from one of our bicycles and rigged it to Frey's treadle sewing machine, so that the sewing machine's footboard turned the flywheel which in turn rotated the dynamo. It worked! While one of us operated the treadle, the others, sitting close by with their books, could read. We made improvements as time went on. Soon, several of our friends had also made one of these contraptions for their household.

During the day, if the weather was nice, we removed the large slab of plywood from the window frame in my room, which was

82

on the sunny side of the street. There we sat together to enjoy the sunshine. One such day, Frey was sitting at a table in front of the window, making a coat for me from an old blanket. My mother was sitting on the other side of the table, reading. I was watching and helping Frey as she was drawing the pattern on the blanket. My brother was away again, back to the hiding place on the boat. Suddenly, outside, a large German truck stopped in front of the apartment block. Soldiers jumped out and an officer started shouting orders. The soldiers, about twenty of them, dispersed and entered the porticos. Some remained on the sidewalk, standing guard. We could see it all clearly underneath us, from the window. The officer stood across the street, watching his men. It was a *razzia*. They were looking for people hiding from the Germans.

"Oh dear," said my mother. "A good thing Folkert isn't here."

Anxiously we watched as the soldiers went from door to door, searching the apartments. We were waiting for them to come to our home. The officer was pacing back and forth across the street. Suddenly he looked up and saw us, and particularly Frey. He crossed the street and stood under our window. He brought his hand to his cap in salute and clicked his heels. He struck up a conversation with Frey, who, like my mother, could speak German reasonably well. After a while he invited himself in for a visit. There was nothing we could do but agree. My mother told me to go to the door and let him in. When I opened the door he was already climbing the stairs of the portico. Some soldiers were with him. He told them to move on, he would check on this one himself. I let him into my room. He smiled at my mother and Frey and took off his cap, looking around for a chair. There were no other chairs in my room, so Mam told me to get one from the kitchen. Then I suddenly remembered the motorcycle.

My room had two hideaway beds, one against each of the opposing walls. They were shaped like a large bookcase, the front closed by a curtain. One bed was not used; the bedspring had been taken out and my father's motorcycle, the Harley-Davidson, had taken its place. The bike was well hidden—as long as no one touched the curtain, which moved when pushed, allowing one of the big handlebars to suddenly appear.

"Oh boy, what if he sees that!" I thought as I returned to my room. The soldier grabbed the chair in my hands and fortunately put it down with the back against the hideaway bed space where the motorcycle was. He stretched his legs, leaned back in the chair, and started talking. I watched, standing by the door. As he talked to Frey, he started to rock the chair on its back legs. Every time the chair leaned back, it touched the curtain and the handlebar of the Harley popped out, close by his ear. I held my breath, but each time he rocked forward again, the curtain closed and the handlebar disappeared.

From where she was sitting, Mam couldn't see it, but Frey threw me a knowing glance before looking away to pick at some imaginary fluff on the blanket that was to become my coat. In and out went the handlebar, as the officer rocked and talked. Frey played along, offering a comment every now and then so as to keep him distracted from what was happening right behind him.

After what seemed like days but was only about half an hour, he looked at his watch and stood up. He clicked his heels and put on his cap. I quickly grabbed the chair, just in case he would push it against the curtain. As Frey walked him to the door I remained standing between the curtain and the chair. I heard them say goodbye. He was gone! Frey came back and sank down in her chair. She was quivering and laughing at the same time. Soon after, we saw the small squadron getting back into the truck, the officer waving at us as he climbed into the cab beside the driver. Then the truck drove off.

I didn't think they had caught anyone.

"Phew," said Frey, "that was a close one. If he had seen the Harley, we would have been in a lot of trouble."

We quickly filled Mam in on what had happened. "We have

to do something about that thing," Mam said. "It is too dangerous to keep it here. Next time they come, they might spot it."

A few days later Folkert returned and the incident was discussed at length.

"Well," said Folkert, "I guess we'd better move it to a better hiding place. What about the secret room?"

"No," said Mam, "I don't want it in the house any longer. We have to get rid of it."

"Vader won't be too happy with that when he returns," I grumbled.

"No, he won't, that's true," Mam said pensively. "What else can we do?"

"Let's disassemble it," Folkert suggested. "Then we can hide the parts in the *schuur*. I think Vader would approve of that."

"Hmm...yes, maybe that's the way to go," answered Mam. "Can you do that? Take it apart, I mean?"

"Yes, it shouldn't be too difficult. I'll give it a try. Jan, here"—he pointed at me—"can give me a hand."

For the next two days Folkert and I laboured. Folkert had made a detailed sketch of the motorcycle. As the bolts and nuts were removed, we put them in a little bag with a letter on it. This letter corresponded with a letter on the drawing and showed exactly where they belonged. We removed the wheels, the fenders, the handlebars, the fuel tank, and several other pieces. In the evening, Frey, Mam, Folkert, and I took the parts we had removed down the stairs, around the apartment block, and through the door that led to the narrow alley in which the *schuur* was located. There we hid each part with other items and tarpaulins that were stored in the *schuur*. The heaviest, largest, and most difficult objects were the main frame and the engine, which Folkert did not feel comfortable disassembling. It took all four of us and a lot of straining to carry these pieces down the stairs and move them into the *schuur*. But eventually we got everything packed away and well hidden.

It was a good thing that Mam made us move the Harley out of the house, because about a week later we had another unexpected visit. Frey was away to see her parents and Folkert had gone back to the boat. It was about seven o'clock in the evening. I was sitting at the piano while Mam was turning the pages of a book with piano exercises, looking for a piece she wanted me to play, when suddenly the doorbell rang. At the same time a heavy fist was banging on the door. Startled, we both jumped up, not knowing what to do.

"What's going on? Who can that be?" Mam exclaimed.

I ran to the window and looked outside. A German army truck and a car were parked outside. We had not heard them coming.

"Germans, Moeder!" I shouted to her. "There's a car and an army truck parked outside."

"My God," Mam said with a shaky voice, wringing her hands. "What's happening now?" Just then, the bell rang again, with more banging on the door. "I guess I'd better open the door," Mam stammered. "You stay here!"

Mam went to the door and opened it. Five men pushed themselves into the house. Two were soldiers dressed in regular uniforms. Three wore black uniforms with peaked hats and a swastika on their left sleeve. They carried revolvers stuck in their belts; their collars displayed SS insignia. One of them appeared to be in command; a baton was swinging in his right hand. They all marched in and told Mam and me to stand in the corner of the living room.

"Are you the only ones in this house?" the commanding officer said, addressing Mam. Then, before she could answer, he turned to me, tapping his baton against his leg, and said in a commanding voice, "Where are the others? Are you hiding anybody here?" Then he bent down and put his face close to mine. He stared me in the face and snarled in a whisper, "You have blond hair and blue eyes. You must be a good Aryan boy."

By now I had learned enough of the German language to

understand what he was saying. But I didn't know how to respond. This fellow and the whole situation scared the living daylights out of me. All I could do was shake my head. At the same time I was mystified about his comments about the colour of my hair and eyes. If that meant I was a good Aryan boy (whatever that was supposed to mean), then what was he? Because I couldn't help noticing that he had dark hair and brown eyes. Was he not an Aryan, or was he a bad Aryan? Was it good or bad to be an Aryan?

The man straightened himself and turned around. Swinging the baton behind his back, then holding it with both hands, he looked again at Mam.

"I know what you people have been up to—we already have your husband. You've been hiding enemies of the German Reich. So speak up, where are they? We will search this place and take it apart if we have to."

By now, Mam, although very frightened, had regained some of her composure. "Leave my little boy alone," she yelled. "We have not done anything illegal. We are not hiding anyone. There is just my son and I here, no one else."

The man looked around the room and then said to the other two black-uniformed men, "Search the house! Look everywhere!" To the soldiers he said, "You two stay here and watch the woman and the boy. Shoot them if they try to run away."

Mam and I stood huddled close in the corner, the two soldiers watching us vigilantly. We heard doors open and close, furniture being moved, drawers being pulled out, closets being emptied. After about two hours—it seemed like eternity—the man who had addressed us came back into the room and motioned the two soldiers to follow him. A minute later we heard the front door slam shut and they were gone. I ran to the window and saw the truck and the car start up and leave.

"They're gone, Moeder," I yelled, watching the vehicles gain speed as they drove away.

"Thank heavens," Mam mumbled, as she sat down in a chair. "First my husband—and now they're after us. I don't know what to do anymore. Maybe we will have to hide too."

She came over to me and put her arms around me. We stood like that for a while, still trembling with fear. Then she straightened herself and with one arm still around me, we both started walking through the rooms of the house, taking stock of the chaos they had left behind. She patted me on the head and said, "Come on, help me straighten out this mess."

We both got busy putting things back where they belonged. The work comforted us. Fortunately, nothing had been broken or damaged. Mam commented that obviously we had done a good job hiding the entrance to the secret room, because the invaders had not found it. If they had, we would have been in a lot of trouble. It was also a blessing that Folkert had not been with us at the time; otherwise, they surely would have taken him away.

12

Meanwhile, I had started school again: at the MULO on Bloem-
fontein Straat, within walking distance of our home. At this school
I made a new friend, Lou Huisman. Lou was a bit taller than I.
He had dark hair and a freckled face. He amazed us with his
incredible brain. I guess he had a photographic memory because
all he had to do was glance over the pages of a book before recit-
ing them exactly as they were printed. He even quoted the page
and paragraph numbers. As far as I knew he never did any home-
work. When we had an exam, just prior to the examination he'd
quickly turn the pages of the subject book, then close it and say,
"Okay, I'm ready." He always passed with flying colours.

Lou excelled in every subject, and amazed the math teacher.
The teacher often wrote a mathematical problem on the blackboard and then asked one of the students to solve it. This usually
meant going to the blackboard and jotting down the various equa-
tions until the right solution was arrived at. Not so with Lou, who
simply gave the correct answer. When asked to explain, he would
say, "It's logical, that is what it has to be, there is no other answer."
Every time this happened, the teacher shook his head in won-
derment, throwing his hands in the air and saying, "Well, Dr.
Einstein, I promise I won't ask you any more dumb questions."

There was another side to Lou. We were taught foreign languages. German, of course, was taught with much pressure; as a
matter of fact, the teacher who taught it was German. One day

he announced that we would be examined on the material we had learned thus far. As exam day drew closer, several kids expressed their concern. We were all worried about the repercussions if we were unable to pass the exam successfully.

"Don't worry," said Lou. "I'll find a way to stop him."

On the morning of exam day, Lou brought with him a heavy briefcase. He called us over and when we had gathered around him he opened the briefcase and let us examine its contents. It was full of German hand grenades, the ones with the wooden handles and a metal cylindrical gadget on the top. "Here," he said, as he handed them out. "Place these with the handle against the footboard of your desk. When I give the sign, give it a kick and it will fall over, making enough of a disturbance to stop the teacher from proceeding with the exam."

"Where did you get these?" I asked.

"Stole them from the Germans," he replied. The bell rang and we went inside, everyone hiding grenades under their clothing.

Our classroom was the science room. The desks in this room were set up like seating in a theatre, on progressively higher risers. I shared one of the big double desks with Lou. Ours was up high, at the back of the room. We all took our seats when the teacher walked in. He had written several phrases on the blackboard. We were to translate them into German and write them down on sheets of paper on our desks. The teacher looked at his watch and said, "Begin. You have twenty minutes."

Lou poked an elbow into my side and kicked the grenade at his feet. I did the same. It was the sign! Promptly the other kids followed. The grenades tumbled off the footboards onto the floor, rolling down the stairs and toward the front of the classroom.

"What in the world is this?" the teacher yelled. "Where did these things come from?"

When he picked one up and saw what it was, he quickly told us to get out of the room. In a short time the whole school was evacuated. When it was eventually learned that Lou was the instigator, he received a reprimand from the principal, but since he was such an excellent student no further action was taken. In any event, the exam had been delayed.

When I talked to Lou later that day and mentioned that it had been a great success, he said, "Yes, but I don't understand why none of them exploded." I laughed—he was kidding, of course! Or so I thought at the time.

One day I met him going into the school carrying a cardboard box. "What's in it?" I asked.

"Erasers," he said.

"A whole boxful of erasers? Where did you get them?" (Remember, they were scarce.)

"Oh, my father used to run a store that sold stationery and stuff. I found this amongst some of the leftovers."

"Wow, what are you going to do with them?"

"Sell them to the school. I'm going to see the principal."

I was hanging around with some of my other classmates, outside in the playground, when he came back out of the school and told me that he had sold the erasers for a good sum of money. The bell rang; classes were starting. We went inside.

That afternoon, the principal stepped into the classroom and said that he wanted to talk with Lou in his office. Lou left and I didn't see him again until the next day. Then I asked him what the principal wanted.

"Oh, he found out that those erasers actually didn't come from my father's store."

"They didn't? How did you get them?"

He hesitated for a second and then said, "Oh, well, they already belonged to the school."

"They already belonged to the school? How could they? He bought them from you...I don't understand."

"Yeah, well, I took them from the storeroom of the school."

"You mean you stole them from the school and then sold them back again?"

"Yeah, that's right."

"And the principal knew that?"

"Yes, well, he didn't know it at the time, but he found out later, I guess. He probably discovered they were gone when he put the ones I sold him into the storeroom, exactly the same amount. He must keep records of those things."

I didn't know what to say. It was the weirdest plot I had ever heard of. Was he pulling my leg, or was he telling the truth? If it had truly happened, how come he hadn't been expelled from school? Because of his excellent grades? If so, what a strange twist there was in the clever brain of my newfound friend. I remembered his earlier remark about the hand grenades and began to wonder.

After only a few months of operation, the MULO closed, and there was no more school. I lost touch with Lou. After the war, though, my old friend Dick came to visit us in the village we had moved to. He asked me, "Didn't you go to school with a fellow by the name of Lou Huisman?"

"Yes, I did. Why?"

"He is all over the newspapers."

"Is he? Why?"

"He murdered someone."

"What!?"

Dick told me that apparently Lou had a friend whose father had died in a concentration camp. He visited the friend and his mother regularly. One time while Lou was there, the mother, during a moment of stress, said, "I wish I were dead." The next day Lou was back at their house again and offered her a glass of juice. She drank it and died. The drink had had cyanide in it. Lou admitted it freely. He said that he had done it because he liked her and wanted to do her a favour: he made her wish come true!

I checked the newspapers myself and learned that during the trial a consulting psychologist observed that Lou Huisman was a genius in some respects but that he had a total lack of social conscience. He concluded that Lou sincerely believed he was complying with the lady's wish.

Things got tougher and tougher, and not only because of the lack of food, electricity, clothing, and firewood. The biggest problem was paranoia. The Nazi regime was very clever in their way of keeping control over a large, starving population: spies were paid with extra ration tickets. People would turn in their friends for a loaf of bread. You could not trust anyone: not neighbours, not friends, and not even, in some cases, family. Spies were everywhere, and arrests were made regularly in the most unlikely places. People were pulled from lineups at grocery stores. Houses were raided at any time of day or night, the Gestapo tipped off by a neighbour. Once I heard my brother say, "If I am ever told to make a choice and either fight in the front lines or live as a civilian in territory occupied by the Nazis, I'll choose the front lines. At least there I will be able to tell the difference between friend and enemy."

In November 1944, Mam made a decision: she and I would leave the city. Twice more, the Gestapo had searched our house and questioned us about hiding enemies of the Reich. By a stroke of luck, in each instance Folkert had been away. But it had become obvious that the SS was suspicious of us. If they had proof that we had been hiding people in the house, they would arrest Mam and perhaps me as well. In addition, we were faced at every moment with a further reduction in our supply of food. Falsifying our ration tickets had become more and more dangerous; they were now often closely scrutinized.

To help satisfy our hungry stomachs, my mother made potato cakes, potato bread, and potato soup, and sugar beet cakes, sugar beet bread, and sugar beet soup. Some people were eating baked or mashed tulip bulbs. Apparently they had an oniony taste, but some were also poisonous. The meals made from potatoes were good; I especially liked the potato cakes. But I hated the sugar beet stuff. Its burning, acidy sweet taste was awful and made my throat hurt. Even just helping my mother to prepare the beets—cleaning them and chopping them up into little bits—made me want to vomit. The smell of the stuff boiling in the pot was terrible too.

Still, mealtimes were something to look forward to. They became the most important parts of the day. As soon as food was put on the plate it was devoured at great speed and made us long for more. We had all lost a great deal of weight, especially Mam, who kept on saying "I have had enough" while pushing her leftovers onto our plates. Often we would argue about that, but she'd insist and wouldn't take it back.

Away from the big cities, food was more plentiful. Mam decided that she and I would go to Friesland, one of the northern provinces, where there were large farms with livestock and fields of grain. There we had relatives and could find shelter. My brother could not come; even with his faked papers, it would be too risky. But if the two of us left, we could leave our ration tickets with Frey and Folkert. We would find food in the countryside, and they would have a better chance of survival. Folkert could hide in the secret room if the Germans came to search the house again, or both he and Frey—and Beertje, who also had to stay—could go to the farm where the boat was kept.

It would be a long journey as there was no transportation: no cars or buses, not even a bicycle. Mam hoped somehow to get on a train that would take us at least partially in the right direction, even though trains were supposed to be available only to troops and persons on official Nazi business. Accordingly, we arrived at the train station at about eight o'clock in the evening, each of us carrying a small suitcase with essential items. A locomotive with passenger cars stood huffing and puffing at the station. Lots of people were standing on the platform, mostly soldiers and the odd civilian. Mam learned from a bystander that the train was a troop transport bound for Zwolle. The city of Zwolle would put us about halfway toward our destination. Mam grabbed my hand and pulled me into the lineup of soldiers climbing into the passenger cars. Once in, we received some curious glances, but no one objected. The compartment was crowded. Most of the soldiers were standing. All the seats were taken. One soldier, a big guy, looked at my mother and then stood up, offering her his seat. My mother thanked him with a smile and sat down, pulling me beside her. Although tight, there was enough space for both of us to sit down. Our luggage was on our knees. Whistles started blowing, the locomotive chugged and belched a puff of smoke, the cars shook and then started to move as the engine took up the strain. We had done it! *Friesland, here we come!*

13

As the wheels click-clacked over the tracks, the soldiers started to make themselves comfortable. In addition to their rifles, they were each heavily loaded with knapsacks and rolled-up sleeping gear, all carried on their backs. The rifles were put down on the floor or set to rest against a bench or wall, the bundles of sleeping gear and the knapsacks came off, and before long most of the soldiers were stretched out on the floor with their heads nestled on their luggage. Some started singing: "*Unter der Laterne bei dem grossen baum...*" Soon everyone joined in. Mam closed her eyes, her head leaning back against the partition above the seat, softly humming along to the well-known song "Lili Marlene." (Amazingly, in spite of the fighting, this lovely German song became popular around the world during the war, taking on lyrics in different languages.)

A soldier sitting across from us started rummaging through his bag. He pulled out a chocolate bar. I watched intently as he broke it into three pieces. One piece he slid into his mouth, the remaining two pieces he handed to me. Wide-eyed I took the gift and thanked him. I carefully placed one piece into my mother's hand and immediately began to nibble on the other one, savouring each bite. I had not tasted anything that good for a very long time. Mam looked at her treasure, looked at me, and then looked at the grinning soldier. "*Dankeschön*," she said as she brought the chocolate to her mouth.

The soldier muttered something while nodding his head agreeably. He moved slightly forward in his seat, cleared his throat, and asked in German where we were going. The other soldier, the big fellow who had given us his seat, was sitting close by on his knapsack. As my mother cautiously answered by saying that we were going to visit relatives, the big soldier threw her a smile and said, "That is a nice thing to look forward to."

"I guess you are leaving The Hague because of the food shortage?" the other soldier asked.

Mam nodded her head in acknowledgement.

"Yes, you and so many others," the soldier replied.

"This war stinks," the big soldier said. "You may not believe it, but we don't want it, either. We'd all rather go home."

"That's for sure," sighed his comrade.

The conversation continued, about the war and the plight of the common soldier, drawn into the conflict as ordered rather than by choice. Since my command of the German language wasn't as good as my mother's, I lost track and instead concentrated on the next piece of chocolate that was handed to me. But as it was melting in my mouth I started to think about the part of the conversation I had understood. The soldiers' comments raised some questions in my mind. Until now I had thought that soldiers were just soldiers. It had never occurred to me that under the uniforms were ordinary people, just like us—but people who had been ordered to fight, to kill other people. Someone else was making them do these awful things. But how was that possible? How could anyone in authority have so much power and not be put in prison? Until now I had thought that all Germans were bad people. But these two guys seemed nice. They had given us chocolate, they had offered us a seat, they had been friendly. What about all the other German people? Were they too actually good people, just like us? The thought was a revelation to me.

The train had now left the city and we were travelling through the countryside. Everything was dark, including the inside of the train, as all lights were off so as to not draw attention. We moved slowly. Every so often we came to a halt and stood quietly on a side track while another train passed from the opposite direction. At other times we stood still and waited for reasons not known to us. We passed through several towns and villages. We dozed off for short stretches and woke up each time the train stopped. During some of the stops more soldiers entered the carriages. The sky started to lighten when we went through another city. The train didn't stop in the large station we went through.

"I think that was Arnhem," I heard my mother say. "We must have been rerouted; we're going in the wrong direction." Concerned, she stood up and looked intently through the window, watching the dark silhouettes of buildings disappearing behind us. The train gained speed as it moved away from the city.

I could tell by her reaction that something was amiss. I knew where we were supposed to be going: to Friesland. I had been there before, but I had only the vaguest idea about how to get there. Apparently Arnhem wasn't on our route.

Mam turned to the big soldier. "Where is this train going? I was told it was going to Zwolle."

The soldier shook his head. "Zwolle? I don't think so. We are going to Germany and then on to the eastern front."

"To Germany? To the eastern front?" Mam was agitated.

Now I was worried too. "What do we do, Moeder?" I asked.

"We have to get off this train somehow," she replied. "But how?" she added, mainly speaking to herself. She returned to her seat, a frown on her forehead.

The answer came some twenty minutes later when suddenly, over the noise made by the train, there was the sound of an explosion. A soldier opened a window and now we could hear the high-pitched noise of diving planes dropping bombs, the screaming howl of their engines punctuated by the rapid report of machine guns fired from the planes. We were being attacked by Allied planes! Abruptly, the train came to a stop. Doors opened and the soldiers poured out, some grabbing their luggage, others leaving it behind. The two soldiers who had been talking to my mother grabbed us both and pushed us to an exit. "Run!" they yelled. "Get away from the train." We both ran as fast as we could, stumbling, tripping, almost falling, down the railway embankment. Then out across a field toward a grove of trees and shrubs we went, the suitcases swinging behind us, mine banging against my legs. We could see soldiers running across the field, also looking for places to hide; some had crawled under the railroad carriages. All this while the deafening roar of the diving planes and rapid fire of machine guns echoed through the early morning air. Then another explosion: sand and rocks and other debris fell down around us. We fell down in a hollow in the ground among the bushes and the trees, my mother covering us with our suitcases.

Then the sound of the planes slowly faded into the distance, their mission accomplished. We crawled out of our hiding place and saw flames coming from some of the train carriages. "Come, let's go," Mam said. She dusted off her coat and then brushed the dirt off my clothing. "There, are you okay?" Without waiting for an answer she gave me my suitcase and grabbed my other hand. We quickly distanced ourselves from the train. Behind us we could hear the shouting of commands: chaos ending, order being restored.

When we cleared the stretch of bushes and trees that bordered the field, we came upon a paved road. In the faint light of early morning we could see the dark silhouette of a house in the distance. It looked like a small farm. "That's east," Mam said. "That is the direction we will take. We haven't gone as far east as Zwolle yet."

We started walking, I carrying my suitcase in one hand with the other one firmly held by my mother.

"Mam, how do you know that's east?" I asked.

"Because the sky is lighter over there," she answered. "That is where the sun is rising. If you always keep in mind that the sun rises in the east and goes down in the west, it will help you know which way you're going." Then she continued, "When you stand with the east to your right and the west to your left, then straight ahead of you is north and behind you is south."

"Is that how ships navigate on the ocean?" I asked.

"Yes, that is more or less how it works—" She stopped abruptly. "You see that?"

I looked and saw that some people had suddenly appeared. Perhaps they had been hiding along the side of the road, or they had come from the farm.

"They must have been watching the air attack," Mam said.

As we approached we saw that the group consisted of two boys in their late teens, one girl about my age, and a man and a woman, probably the parents. They watched us as we came closer. We were now within talking distance.

"Did you come from that train?" the man asked.

We both nodded. The others did not say anything. The woman looked us over carefully, scanning our suitcases, wrinkled clothing, and faces. She turned to her husband and whispered something in his ear. The husband nodded his head. "Right," he said, looking at Mam. "You'd better come with us." He extended his hand to Mam and said, "My name is van Hoorn and this is my wife; my two boys, Henk and Freddie; and Annie, our little one." Mam shook hands with the van Hoorns and introduced herself and me. After the formalities were over, Mr. van Hoorn said, "Good, now let's start moving. This isn't over yet; those planes may come back, and soon there will be German trucks and who knows what else to collect those soldiers. Henk, you take the lady's suitcase, and Freddie, you take the one from the boy." The boys grabbed our luggage.

"We live just over there," the woman said, pointing to the farmhouse. "That must have been quite an ordeal, being on that train. You look tired and must be hungry."

The van Hoorn farmhouse, year unknown. The van Hoorns might have given this picture to Mam when we were there; she kept it in the jewellery box with Pa's letters.

As we were walking, my mother between the two adults, and I following, flanked by Freddie, Henk, and Annie, we learned that indeed they had been watching the air attack. Apparently they had just finished milking their cows when they heard the noise of the planes and the explosions. "You came just in time for breakfast," Henk said, throwing me a jovial smile from his round face. He waved Mam's suitcase in the direction of the house which was now only a short distance away. Freddie's face was thinner, more serious. He must be the older one, I thought.

The family were dressed in the usual Dutch country garb. The boys wore dark blue long pants, held up by suspenders over their shirts. Each wore a heavy jacket and a tweed cap covering pale blond hair. Annie and her mother wore long dark skirts reaching down to their ankles. The mother wore a jacket loose over her shoulders, the sleeves hanging empty. Annie wore a full-length coat. Her hair, two thick blond braids, reached down almost to her waist. The open front of the mother's jacket revealed a white blouse with lots of embroidered flowers in various colours. Her hair was a darker blond, tied in a bun at the back. The father wore brown wool pants and a dark grey, heavy tweed jacket. He also had blond hair which showed under his tweed cap. All of them wore *klompen*—wooden shoes. And all of them were quite tall, like my mother, except Annie, who was about my height.

I looked at my own plus-fours (baggy pants that gathered below the knees), woollen socks, and leather shoes protruding from under the long coat made by Frey from a blanket, and at my mother's skirt, stockings, and knee-length coat with fox fur on the collar. I realized that although our clothing was worn and somewhat shabby, to them we would be readily identified as city slickers.

As we entered the house we could hear the sound of trucks approaching: army trucks destined for the wreckage we had left behind. We entered the house through a side door that led into a large kitchen. At the centre stood a long table with chairs around it. A cooking stove exuded a comfortable heat from along one of the long walls. It was flanked by a long counter with a granite countertop and wooden cabinets under and above. In one of the corners stood a massive wooden chopping block on four legs; above it were shelves with Delft Blue plates and cups and saucers. The floors were flagstone, scrubbed squeaky clean. The window-sills were crowded with potted geraniums showing their bright red flowers. It was a welcoming sight, the geraniums in particular because at our house in The Hague we had lots of geraniums too. They bloomed all year and were my mother's pet project, even during the war.

"Sit down at the table," Mrs. van Hoorn said. "Make yourselves comfortable while I make a pot of tea."

She busied herself by the stove where a large kettle sat steaming. Mr. van Hoorn pulled a chair from the table and offered it to Mam. I sat down beside her.

"Come here, Annie," said Mrs. van Hoorn, "and set the table for me." She pulled a folded tablecloth from one of the cupboards and gave it to Annie.

Mr. van Hoorn, Freddie, and Henk had seated themselves at the table. As soon as Annie had everything in place, Mrs. van Hoorn deposited a large teapot on the table while Annie fetched a jar with sugar and a pitcher with milk.

"How do you like your tea?" Mrs. van Hoorn asked Mam. "Sugar, milk?"

"Yes, please. A little sugar and some milk."

"What about you, young man? Tea? Or would you rather have a glass of milk?"

"Yes, please, milk, please." I eagerly received the glass from her hands. I hadn't tasted real milk for a long time.

"Good for you. Milk makes you strong. Especially this, it's straight from the cow. My boys drink milk too and so does Annie."

As she poured a cup of tea for her husband, she said to Mam, "You go ahead, drink while it's hot, and help yourself if you want more. In the meantime I'll get breakfast ready."

"Can I help?" asked Mam.

"No, no, you can just relax. Annie and I have everything under control."

Mam sipped her tea. I gulped down the delicious milk. Mr. van Hoorn quietly watched us while softly blowing in his cup to cool his tea. Annie had gone back to help her mother. Freddie looked at my empty glass and said, "Done already? Want some more?" Without waiting for a reply he brought over the pitcher and refilled my glass. Henk was watching me as I brought the glass to my mouth. "Good, isn't it?" he said. "You must be thirsty, and hungry, too, I bet. Was there no food on the train?"

"No," I answered. "I had some pieces of chocolate, though. One of the soldiers gave it to me." And then both Henk and Freddie started questioning me about the train, the soldiers, and the air raid. "What was it like? Were you scared? How come you were on that train? How come the soldiers gave you chocolate? They were Germans, weren't they?"

As I tried to answer their questions, Annie put a plate with sliced bread on the table—a whole loaf—and next to it, an earthenware dish filled with butter. Then Mrs. van Hoorn put down a large plate with fried eggs; I had heard them sizzle on the stove and my mouth was watering ferociously. This was followed by crispy slices of bacon, which I knew were coming because I had been savouring the aroma as it spread through the kitchen. I couldn't believe it, but there it was, right in front of my eyes. A table full of delicious food, the likes of which I hadn't seen or tasted for a long time. No sugar beet pie, no potato cakes, no tulip bulb mash; instead, real eggs, real bacon, delicious bread with real butter. And...milk! Lots of it!

Mrs. van Hoorn pulled out her chair and sat down opposite Mam, and Annie sat down next to her across from me. "Let's have a moment of quiet, boys," Mrs. van Hoorn said.

Mam nudged me and put a finger to her lips. "Shh," she whispered. I looked at her and understood. We were not churchgoing people, but when we were at my grandparents' they always said a prayer before and after meals.

The room fell silent; everyone closed their eyes and folded their hands. I did too but couldn't help sneaking a peek through one slitted eye, and noticed Annie doing the same. When I caught her eye she quickly squeezed her eyes shut again.

Mr. van Hoorn prayed. "Thank you, Lord, for what we are about to receive..." More words followed, but they were mumbled and difficult to understand. In any event, I wasn't really listening to the words. I was intently focused on the eggs and bacon and bread with butter. Then Mr. van Hoorn said, *"Eet smakelijk"* ("Enjoy your meal"), and the eating could begin. I knew I would have no trouble enjoying this meal.

While we were eating Mam explained why we had left our

home. She told the van Hoorns what had happened to Pa, about my brother, back at home with our ration tickets, and that we were on our way to Friesland. They all listened without interruption. When Mam had finished, Mrs. van Hoorn said, "What a terrible ordeal. You must be very worried about your husband."

"Yes," Mam replied, "and I'm also worried about my son. I hope he won't be caught by the Nazis too." There was a short silence, and then she continued, "However, we have to keep our hopes up and make the best of it." Looking at me she added, "Don't we, Jan?" I couldn't answer because I had just stuffed another big bite of food into my mouth.

Mr. van Hoorn pulled out his pocket watch and looked at it. "You know," he said, "I have an idea. Soon, the milk truck will come by to pick up the milk from the farms in this area."

I remembered noticing several large metal milk canisters sitting by the road in front of the house when we had arrived earlier.

"The milk truck," Mr. van Hoorn continued, "takes the milk to Zutphen, to the processing plant. I know the driver well, and I could ask him to take you along. That would be another thirty-some kilometres in the right direction."

"That would be wonderful," Mam said. "It saves us a lot of walking."

"Well, we'd better get ready, then," Mrs. van Hoorn said. "The milk truck will be here soon. Have you had enough to eat? I'll make some sandwiches for you to take along." She stood up and went back to the kitchen counter. Annie and my mother started clearing the table. I quickly finished the last morsels on my plate. Henk and Freddie followed their father as he left the house. A few minutes later we heard the sound of the truck. I went outside to look and saw Mr. van Hoorn talking to the driver. "Call your mother," he yelled at me over the sound of the truck's engine. "The driver is in a hurry, but he'll take you both."

We quickly thanked the van Hoorns for their hospitality

and said goodbye. Mam and Mrs. van Hoorn were locked in an embrace when Mr. van Hoorn said, "Hurry, the driver is waiting."

We climbed into the cab next to the driver and waved goodbye as we drove away.

"Such nice people," Mam said, wiping a tear from her face.

14

It was evening by the time we arrived in the city of Zutphen. The truck had made many stops, picking up milk canisters at the various farms. The truck driver was a nice man, but not much of a talker. When Mam asked him something he would give a short reply and then return to silence. We never did learn his name. He did tell us that there was a place in Zutphen, an empty school, that provided shelter for people like us. It had been organized by some of the local citizens. He said that it was on his route and he would drop us off there.

It was dark, cold, and raining when we drove through the outskirts of the city. There was no heater in the truck. I had my coat tightly wrapped around me, hands in my pockets, but I was still shivering. Mam was cold too; she had her hands inside her coat sleeves and the fur collar over her mouth and up to her nose. We were now driving along a tree-lined road. It was very dark; not even the truck had lights.

As with houses, at night no cars, trucks, or motorcycles were allowed to show any lights. Their headlights were covered except for a little slit that let through only enough light to show the surface of the road just ahead to the driver. This was closely monitored by the Germans. They didn't want any lights to be seen during the night for fear of air attacks. Any Allied planes overhead could zero in on the lights and use them as a beacon, a confirmation of their position, or a target for their bombs.

Suddenly the truck came to a stop. The driver pointed to a building surrounded by a fence. "That is the school," he said. "Go through the gate to the front door—there will be people there." We thanked him, opened the door, grabbed our suitcases, and stepped down from the cab. Cold and stiff from sitting in cramped quarters for such a long time, we hobbled through the pouring rain to the entrance of the school. The door was closed but not locked. Mam opened it and looked inside. Just inside were some women in a wide hallway. One of them approached us and pointed down the hallway to the gym. It was full of people, some sitting down at tables, others lined up at a table in the far corner. There were pots and dishes there and four women were serving. We joined the line and waited for our turn for a bowl of soup and two slices of bread. Thankfully we accepted the food and sat down at one of the tables.

There must have been close to a hundred people there, mostly women and children, some elderly people, all of them on the move, leaving the cities and going to the countryside in search of food and shelter.

Across from us at our table was a woman with three little children, one boy about seven years old and twin girls, about four. With them was an elderly couple, the woman's parents. They were all from Rotterdam. The woman's home had been destroyed by bombing during the first days of the war, and her husband killed. She herself had been injured, which resulted in the twins being born prematurely while she was being treated. The boy had been with his grandparents at the time and therefore managed to escape the ordeal. They had walked all the way from Rotterdam and had been on the road a little over two months.

"It's just terrible in the city," the woman said, "although now sometimes I wonder what is worse, dying from hunger in Rotterdam or..." She looked up pensively and then continued. "This trip is so hard on my parents, and especially with my two little girls, we are having a tough time covering any distance. I had a buggy in which the two little ones could sit but it broke down some time ago. One of the axles broke and the wheels came off. Fortunately, we managed to find a pushcart in which the girls sit, and often little Jaapie"—she pointed to the little boy—"gets to ride in it too. My father and I take turns pushing the thing. We can only do it for about half an hour at a time, then we have to take a break and rest."

Mam and I listened as the woman talked. Her parents didn't say anything. Her mother was looking ahead of her with a vacant stare. The father, whose own soup bowl had been emptied, was absently feeding the little girl sitting on his knee. The other twin was sitting with her mother, also being spoon-fed. The boy, Jaapie, had finished his food and was fast asleep, his head on the table.

"Where are you going?" Mam asked.

"To Rijssen, or at least close to it. I have a sister who lives there. She and her husband have a farm not too far from Rijssen. They invited us to come. Their house is a bit small to accommodate all of us, so it will be a little crowded, but as long as there is food and a stove that produces warmth...that's all we can ask for."

"That is quite a story," Mam said. "Rijssen isn't far from here—I would guess another thirty-five kilometres. You're getting close."

"Yes, and their farm is before Rijssen, so a few more days and we'll have finished this terrible journey."

Mam looked around at the other people sitting at the various tables or lined up at the food counter. "I bet every one of them has a story to tell," she whispered.

We spent the night on the floor of the gym. One of the charity ladies brought us a blanket under which I snuggled close to Mam.

Early the following day we were on the road again, heading north in the direction of Zwolle. The road was on the dike that ran along the river IJssel. Fortunately, it had stopped raining. Many other people were on the road, some of them pushing carts loaded with their belongings. As we progressed, the road became more crowded with people, some of them going in the opposite direction but most heading for Zwolle. Occasionally we talked to some of them. Most came from the big cities: The Hague, Rotterdam, Amsterdam; some from Arnhem and Nijmegen. Sometimes we had to wait along the side of the road to let German troop transports pass. We walked and walked and walked. My feet started to hurt from the blisters on my heels and toes. Mam had the same problem but she never complained. When I started dragging behind, Mam would say, "*Door zetten, Jan, niet opgeven.*" ("Persevere, Jan, don't give up.")

Sometimes, Allied aircraft would dive down and attack the troop transports. The result became familiar: people yelling and screaming, scattering off the road, leaving their carts, or hiding underneath them; panic, chaos! We would run off the road too and lie down by the side of the dike, our suitcases covering our heads, hoping we wouldn't get hit by the gunfire. Often we heard people cry out that they had been hit by a bullet or shrapnel. After one of these attacks, we walked past a woman pushing a cart on which, among suitcases and other luggage, lay a motionless child, its clothes covered with blood that had gone dark brown and dull. Mam pulled me along. "Don't look," she said. But I couldn't help staring. It looked unreal, as if a doll in dirty clothes had been thrown on the cart. And as I kept looking back, the woman pushing the cart became impressed on my memory. She kept looking straight ahead, her face without expression, as if she were somewhere else. For the longest time she kept appearing before me, usually in the night, during a bad dream. I knew I'd never forget that woman's face.

Rockets, V1s or V2s, kept flying over our heads too. Someone said they were being fired at Antwerp and that they were launched not far away from us. Whenever one was heard or seen, we'd pay close attention to it. If the roaring sound of the rocket suddenly stopped, it meant the thing had failed and would come tumbling down. When that happened, everyone scattered and hid by the side of the dike. It occurred to me that in London and Antwerp, or wherever they were destined for, people would be happy when a rocket failed, but for us it was the other way around. We breathed a sigh of relief when it kept going on its way.

When we were hungry we stopped at farms, my mother offering housework in exchange for food. Some farms kept their doors tightly shut or had signs saying that they could not help. At other places we were fed without hesitation. At some places Mam scrubbed floors or did the laundry. When she did the laundry, scrubbing the clothes on a contoured metal plate that was on the side of a large metal tub filled with soap and water, I helped her with the wringer. Mam fed the cleaned clothing in between the rollers while I cranked the handle, water draining from the material as it was being squeezed through the rollers. We slept in barns and haystacks.

The distance from Zutphen to Zwolle via the winding road along the river is about ninety kilometres. On foot it felt more like three thousand kilometres. After several days, I forget how many, we reached Deventer, another city along our route. There again, we found a shelter set up by volunteers. Mam helped with the food preparation and we were allowed to stay for a couple of days, to rest and let the blisters on our feet heal a bit. Then we hit the road again. The blisters were not quite gone and before long our feet started to hurt again. Each step hurt. My socks were worn through and the remains stuck to the sores. Whenever we were close enough to the river, we bared our feet and stuck them into the icy cold water. That gave momentary relief at least. Often we saw other people dangling their feet into the water.

Our progress became slower and slower. Finally we reached Zwolle, where we recuperated for a few days with some people who were acquaintances of my parents. We couldn't stay too long because they were also having a tough time with the food shortage. However, the time there allowed our feet to heal a bit more. Someone cut the toes out of my shoes because they were too small. The openings gave much relief. The soles were quite worn, too, but nothing could be done about that.

15

We left Zwolle and headed for Meppel, another twenty-five kilometres or so to the north. Much of the same, walk, walk, walk,
but not as many people on the road this time. For a short stretch
we got lucky and got a ride from a farmer in his horse-drawn
wagon. He took us to his farm where we spent five days working
in exchange for food and board. Mam helped the farmer's wife by
cleaning and scrubbing, and by mending socks, while I cleaned
the barn, fed the pigs, and brought hay for the cows.

After that, back on the road again, walk, walk, walk, sleeping in haystacks or among the bushes. We passed Meppel, then
smaller towns and villages, and eventually, after many, many
days, we were in the province of Friesland. The farms were much
bigger here: big farmhouses, very well kept, and wide fields with
lots of cows.

At one of those farms we were welcomed with open arms.
"We can use a good strong woman like you," Mrs. Hiemstra, the
farmer's wife, said. "You and your boy can stay here as long as you
like." After being introduced to her husband and sons, we were
shown to a room with a *bedstee*. A *bedstee* is a bed that is built into
a cupboard in a wall. Open two doors and there is the bed, large
enough for two. "There is the bathroom," Mrs. Hiemstra said,
"and over there is a closet. Put down your luggage and freshen up.
When you're done, join me in the kitchen." She left us standing
in the room.

The Hiemstra farm in 2006.—AUTHOR PHOTO

"Well," Mam said, "maybe we should stay here. They seem like nice people. We are close, but it is still about another twenty kilometres to Heerenveen, and we are both tired. Besides, who knows what other obstacles we will run into on the way there." We had planned to go and stay with my cousin Pia. She was married to Sjaak Batstra, a member of the Marechaussee, a police force somewhat similar to the Canadian RCMP.

"Anyway," Mam continued, "Pia and Sjaak probably have their own problems. With their three little children they have lots of mouths to feed. Heerenveen is a fairly large place and food is likely a challenge there too. So, we'll stay here for now and see what the future brings." Having said that, she opened one of the suitcases and started to remove its contents.

I was happy with my mother's decision. No more walking on sore feet, no more carrying of heavy luggage, no more diving into roadside holes and bushes to avoid Allied gunfire aimed at

German patrols, no more wondering if we would find a safe and dry spot to sleep. No more empty stomach crying out for something to eat.

It was three o'clock in the afternoon when we entered the kitchen. Everyone was seated around a large table. "Have a seat," Mrs. Hiemstra invited us, "and have a cup of tea. Help yourself." Cups and saucers and a large teapot were on the table. There was also a big plate of raisin buns, a chunk of cheese, and a dish of butter. Mam poured us a cup of tea while I looked from the raisin buns to Mrs. Hiemstra.

"Go ahead, young man," she said with a big smile. "Make sure you put some butter on it."

The three sons, ranging in age from about twenty to twenty-five, watched me with interest while Mr. and Mrs. Hiemstra questioned Mam about our trip. She explained why we had left The Hague, about Pa having been arrested and put into a concentration camp, and about not knowing what would become of Folkert.

"You are fortunate," Mam said. "You still have your husband and sons with you."

"Yes," the Hiemstras replied, "so far we have been lucky, but we don't know what will happen next around here, either. Until now the Germans have left us alone because we operate a farm and they need our produce. But several men from other farms have been taken to German labour camps."

The three sons had been paying close attention to the conversation. Every now and then, one of them interrupted to get a further explanation about some of the things that had happened to us. Suddenly Arie, the youngest, who was sitting next to me, pushed his chair back and said, "Wow, those shoes of yours are well worn. There's not much left! It's time you got rid of those things. Come with me. You are going to be a farm boy now; I'll get you some real footwear."

He stood up, grabbed my hand, and said, "Follow me." I

tagged along behind him as he left the kitchen, stepped outside, and then went into a large shed. Once inside, I looked around in amazement. I had expected to be in a barn with animals, but instead this place was filled on one side with neatly stacked, large chunks of wood. On the other side was a workbench with an assortment of tools, mainly large metal rods with a handle at one end and a chisel-like, curved blade at the other.

"Welcome to my workshop," Arie said. "Sit down on this stool here, so I can take some measurements. Take your shoes off and put your feet on this wooden board." Arie produced a pencil and marked the circumference of my feet on the board. "Ah, such small feet," he said. "Won't take long to get you fixed up." He walked over to the stacks of wood chunks and selected two pieces. He carried them over to the workbench and picked up a tool that had a sharp, slightly curved steel blade with wooden handles at both ends. He started cutting, slicing, and shaping.

"I make the best *klompen* in Friesland," Arie said proudly. "People come from all over to get my clogs. Make them from willow wood. That's all that stuff you see piled up there." He threw a glance in the direction of the stacks of lumber. "I'm beginning to run low on supplies. Will have to go and get some more pretty soon." He glanced back at me and suggested, "You can come with me and help. The willows I need grow along the edges of the ditches and canals; they're called knot willows. It's the best wood for this purpose: soft and easy to work with, doesn't split when it dries, has no knots, and wears well on the feet."

Arie explained, "The knot willow gets its name because at the top of its trunk it has a large knot out of which the branches grow. Below the knot, the main trunk is straight and has no branches; therefore there are no knots in that part of the tree. The chunks of wood which I have piled up over there"—Arie looked at the woodpile again—"all come from the main trunks of the trees."

As Arie talked and busied his hands with the tools, the chunks of wood began to take shape. Soon two wooden shoes, with gently curved tops and sharply curved points at the toes, were sitting side by side on the workbench.

"Right, that's done. Now we have to hollow them out and fit them to your feet."

He put one of the clogs in a receptacle on the floor and chose another tool from his collection. With turning motions he started to slice and carve the inside of the clog. Every once in a while he put his hand inside and felt the curvature with his fingers. This he alternated with an occasional look at and feel of my feet followed by some more carving and scraping. I was fascinated by the process and hardly noticed the two hours that passed until he asked me to put my feet into the clogs.

"How does that feel?" he asked. "Tell me where it feels uncomfortable so that I can make adjustments."

After a bit more scraping, I was walking around in the shed in my brand new clogs. They were a perfect fit and extremely comfortable.

"There you go," Arie said. "Now you can throw those old shoes into the garbage. You won't need them anymore. Welcome to the Hiemstra farm."

I couldn't believe what had just happened. A pair of brand new clogs! These weren't my first; Pa and I always wore clogs when working in the garden. They kept one's feet dry and cozy, especially in winter with an extra pair of thick woollen socks, or with some hay stuffed into them. But these clogs were special. Never had I had clogs that were made to measure—made especially for me, by this complete stranger! I stared at my feet, at my new footwear, tears welling in my eyes. Impulsively I stepped forward and wrapped my arms around Arie, burying my head against his chest.

"That's okay, little fella," Arie said, patting me on my head. "You have had some rough times, but things will get better from now on."

The clogs Arie had made for me were weekday, working clogs.

Later he made me a pair of clogs to be worn on Sundays and special occasions. Those were varnished and decorated with flowers and fancy trimmings.

The Hiemstra farmhouse was a huge building with a tiled roof. The living quarters were in the front, and the barn was in the back. The kitchen was behind the living quarters and behind it was the dairy, where they made cheese and butter. In the back of the dairy was a door that opened to the barn. Each day, in the wee hours of the morning, the cows were brought from the fields and led into the barn for milking. I helped each morning to round up the cows from the fields. This was not a difficult job because the cows knew exactly what to expect. Calmly, as soon as they saw us, they would walk toward the holding pen, their udders bulging with milk and swinging left and right, in rhythm with their steps. About twenty of them were then led inside the barn where each one was tied to a pole. Sitting beside—almost under—a cow, on small one-legged wooden stools with metal pails between their knees, Mr. Hiemstra and his sons would start milking. As soon as the cow was milked, the person milking would pick up his stool, empty the pail into a large container and move on to the next cow. It soon became my job to untie the milked cow, lead her out of the barn into the field, and return with a new cow from the holding pen.

When the milking was done, the big milk containers were loaded onto a cart and taken to the road in front of the house where, later, they would be picked up by a dairy company for processing. I tried but couldn't load the heavy jugs onto the cart, but I did help pull the cart to the road. After all this was done, it was time for breakfast, which had been prepared by Mrs. Hiemstra and Mam. Bacon, eggs, thick slices of home-baked bread, and fresh butter, all prepared at the farm. It was a real feast!

It also became my job, each day after breakfast, to gather the eggs from the chicken coop and put them in the dairy. The Hiemstras didn't have many chickens, just enough to keep the family supplied with eggs. The chickens roamed freely through the yard and one day, quite by accident, I discovered that one chicken for some reason laid her eggs under a hedge in the front garden rather than in the coop. When I told Mrs. Hiemstra, she said, "Well, I'll be—isn't that something. I wondered why that chicken wasn't laying eggs. Good thing you found that out—I was planning to put it into the oven and roast it for dinner. I guess now that will have to wait." I was glad that I had saved the chicken's life. From then on, I made sure to check the bird's secret hiding place daily.

I had lots of other chores to do at the farm. Mam was busy too. She helped with all the household duties, including making cheese and butter. The cheeses were stacked on shelves in the dairy to cure and age. Most of them would be sold. Most of the butter was sold too. It was kept in a cellar below the dairy and was picked up regularly, together with the cheese, by storekeepers from nearby villages. A lot of it, I think, went to the Germans.

Even with all my chores, I had plenty of time to do other things. I soon started making friends with kids from neighbouring farms. Two of them, both boys of my age, were relatives of the Hiemstras and they came to visit frequently. Hanging out with them helped me to pick up the Frisian language in a very short time.

Friesland has its own language. Some people say it is a dialect but that isn't true. It's definitely another language that goes back to the days of the Vikings. There is some resemblance to the Dutch language but it also has a lot in common with English. The phrase *"Brea, bûter, en griene tsiis is goed Ingelsk en goed Frysk"* is a good example; it is pronounced almost the same way as the English translation: "Bread, butter, and green cheese is good English and good Fries." Frisian variants are also spoken in Groningen, the neighbouring province to the east, and in northwestern parts of Germany. In some areas of England where Vikings settled long ago, people speak a dialect closely related to Frisian. "Fries" has many similarities to Danish too—another Viking connection.

All people in Friesland can speak Dutch because that's what is learned in school, but they normally speak Frisian to each other. It became so normal for me to speak Frisian that often when I spoke to Mam, she would have to stop me, saying, "Speak Dutch, or I can't understand you."

There were horses on the Hiemstra farm too: four of them. They were used for pulling a large cart and a plow. Two horses were needed to pull the plow. But when Arie and I went looking for wood for the clogs, we needed one horse to pull the wagon. I enjoyed going with Arie. He had become my best pal, and we were always doing things together: reorganizing and cleaning his workshop, selecting and cutting knot willows. He had a big saw that we used to cut the trees, he pulling on the saw at one end, I pulling on the other. The willows were not tall, only about two to two and a half metres, but they were thick and it took quite a while to cut through them. When one was down we cut it into pieces about thirty centimetres long and then loaded the pieces onto the wagon. Back home we removed the bark, and then usually Arie sliced them in half and squared them off. They were then stacked inside where they could dry. This had to be done carefully, because Arie didn't want them to dry too much. Dry willow was difficult to work with. He inspected his woodpile regularly, and sometimes sprayed water over it.

The horse Arie used to pull the wagon was a nice old guy, who liked to nuzzle me with his nose. The other horses were black; this one was brown with white stockings. He was a Gelderlander with a huge furry body and big feet. His name was Bruin.

"He likes you," Arie said when one day he caught me petting and talking to Bruin. "Have you ever ridden a horse?"

"No," I answered. "Never."

"Well, then, it's about time that you do." He grabbed a halter and put it over Bruin's head. "Come here, I'll help you up." He grabbed me by my waist and lifted me onto the horse. "Just hold on to his mane and I'll walk him around."

Arie started leading Bruin while holding on to the halter. After a walk of about ten metres he let go of the halter and kept walking. Bruin followed him calmly. "There, you see, that's all there is to it. Bruin will take care of you. If you want to stop all you have to say is 'ho.' Try it!"

Imitating Arie's husky voice, I said, "Ho," and Bruin stopped on the spot.

"Now pat him on the neck and say 'good boy.'" I did as I was told, and Arie said, "Good. Now give him a little tap on the side with your right foot, like so." He grabbed my right foot and tapped it against Bruin, who promptly started walking again.

"There you go. Now you can ride. Tomorrow we have to take all the horses to the blacksmith for shoeing. You can take Bruin."

I could hardly wait for tomorrow to come; I didn't sleep much that night in anticipation of the ride to the blacksmith.

The next day, after the early morning chores were done and we had finished breakfast, Arie gathered the horses. Two were harnessed to the front of the cart, the third one was attached to the back with a lead line, and Bruin stood alone. I was lifted onto his back. Bruin had done this many times before and knew exactly where we were going. I held on to his mane and then, as I became more comfortable, I let go and patted and stroked him. I think Bruin enjoyed this because every time I patted him, he swung his huge head sideways and made that lip-flapping noise that horses like to make when they are contented—*brrph*.

The blacksmith was waiting for us when we arrived in St. Nicolaasga, a small village three or four kilometres away.

"I would like you to do these three first," Arie said to the blacksmith, Gerard. "Then as soon as they are done I can go back to the farm because I have someone coming who needs clogs. When you're done with Bruin, perhaps you can give Jan here a lift up so that he can take him home."

"Sure, no problem," the blacksmith said.

"B-b-but…," I stammered. "I have to go back all alone?"

"That's right," said Arie. "Don't you worry—Bruin knows the way home. Just stay on him. If for some reason you have to get off, then ask somebody to give you a lift back up. Everybody in the village is familiar with horses, so don't be shy to ask for help."

I wasn't too sure about this situation but figured that I would deal with it somehow.

Soon Arie's horses were shod and ready to go. Arie climbed onto the wagon and said, "I'll see you soon." He waved as the cart pulled away down the street.

"Okay, now it's your turn," the blacksmith said, lifting one of Bruin's feet and putting it between his knees. He removed the old shoes and began trimming. A new shoe was heated up in the fire, pounded with a hammer, and shaped. The hot iron sizzled; the pungent smell and smoke of burning hoof enveloped us when for a few seconds it was held against Bruin's hoof to make a perfect fit. Then it was cooled in a bucket of water before being fastened with special nails. "Bruin, my buddy," I murmured while fondly stroking his forehead. The gentle creature remained undisturbed throughout the whole procedure.

In the middle of nailing the shoes, Gerard suddenly stopped and said, "Did you hear that?"

"Yeah," I said. "I thought I heard something, too, like fire-crackers."

"Yes," he said, "bang, bang, bang, bang. It sounded as if it came from the village. Wonder what it was. Oh well, who knows, maybe something fell, or somebody hit something." He went back to his work, but a few minutes later we heard some engine noise and a truck roared past the shop. It was a German army vehicle with soldiers in it. We both walked out of the shop to see where it was going. It was headed out of the village.

"What in the world is going on?" Gerard said, looking toward the village and then again in the direction of the disappearing vehicle. He shrugged his shoulders and went back to work.

A short while later, Bruin's shoes were fitted and securely attached to his feet.

"Okay, the job is done," Gerard said. "Let me help you on your horse and you're on your way home."

Back on top of Bruin, I grabbed his mane and gave a tap with my right foot. Obediently, Bruin started plodding in the right direction. "Goodbye, Mister Blacksmith," I said. "Thank you very much; see you next time." He grinned and gave me a wave back.

The blacksmith shop was located on the far end of the village. To go back to the farm I had to go through the village again before reaching the road that led to the farm. As we approached the village centre I noticed a crowd gathered ahead of us on a village square. As we came closer I could see they were gathered in a circle looking at something on the ground. Then, when closer yet, from my elevated position on Bruin I could see three bodies spread in awkward positions on the pavement of the square: two men and a woman. My heart started pounding as I watched: they were dead, blood flowing from them onto the pavement. It was an awful sight. Surreal! More people started arriving. Unconsciously I brought Bruin to a halt while I stared at the bodies.

I heard one of the people in the crowd say to one of the new arrivals, "The SS brought them here. They shot them right here on the spot and just left them. They said these people were traitors, that they were an insult to the Führer, and they were leaving them here as a warning: to show us what happens when we resist. Then they said '*Sieg Heil*' and the scumbags drove off."

This last remark caused someone to say, "Shush, watch what you're saying or you'll end up like this."

"I know these people," another onlooker said.

Suddenly, a woman who was part of the crowd spotted me sitting on Bruin.

"Hey you," she yelled, "get away from here. This is no place for a child. Go on, go home."

Her words brought me out of my shocked daze. I quickly

prodded Bruin and moved on, out of the village, back on the road to the farm. The rest of the trip was like travelling in a fog. I don't remember getting home, getting off the horse, putting him back in the field with the other horses. Everything was like a dream, a bad dream that will stay with me forever. I can still see those bodies with the blood spilling on the village square.

16

Every evening we gathered in the living room to listen to the news. Most houses had a radio, but it was not a real radio. With the real thing you can search and tune to the station of your choice. The radio that people were allowed in German-controlled territory was a gadget connected directly to the broadcasting station in Hilversum. There was Hilversum 1 and Hilversum 2. You could switch from one station to the other, but no other stations were available. These stations were controlled and monitored by the Germans and broadcast German and Dutch music, news (as interpreted by the Germans), and Third Reich propaganda.

To find out what was really going on, you needed a real radio. But they were illegal, and German patrols constantly checked residential areas for antennas. The Germans also had gadgets with which they could tell if anyone nearby was using a real radio.

Mr. Hiemstra had one, hidden in a secret place under the floor of the living room. For an antenna he used a coil of wire that had to be stretched out and connected to a post outside. After the radio had been removed from its hidden compartment, the antenna connected, and the radio turned on, we would move close to the speaker and listen. One of us had to go to the window regularly and peek out to see if anyone was nearby. We also listened for engine noise in case a patrol vehicle happened by. If anyone noticed something suspicious, a bit of a panic erupted and the radio and its antenna were quickly put away.

It usually took a while to get the radio tuned to Radio Oranje (Radio Orange), a special Dutch broadcast sent by the BBC from England. There was always a lot of interference on the station; the Germans sent out distorting signals to that particular frequency. Sometimes it was so bad that not even constant retuning could make the spoken words understandable. But often we could get a pretty good idea of what was happening in the fight against the Nazis. That station was also used to send messages to the various Resistance forces. The announcer would suddenly utter a phrase that didn't make any sense. It was a code understandable to only the intended recipient.

The radio kept us up to date on the war and liberation efforts. Contrary to what the Germans were saying, their armies were losing on all fronts and were in retreat. Our own Queen Wilhelmina, who had escaped to England, made speeches on this radio station. She told us to hang on, that our suffering would soon be over. We learned the details about D-Day, when Allied troops had a major victory in Normandy, and we followed their progress from there. Canadian troops that had fought battles in France, Belgium, the Scheldt, and Germany were dispatched to the Netherlands to join other Canadians who had fought in Italy. Sent in by parachute, the Canadians fought in Arnhem. After two days of house-to-house fighting the city was finally cleared. We heard that Deventer had been liberated and that the troops were advancing onto Zwolle—the route we had so recently travelled. It was now February 1945, and we hoped that soon we would be liberated too.

After the radio and antenna were put back into the hiding place, it was bedtime. We went to bed early because the work started well before sunrise. This was the time when Mam and I were alone in our room and had time for a private chat. The subject was usually Pa and Folkert. We both worried about them, and as we talked, Mam often suddenly looked away into the distance, tears coming to her eyes. Then I would cuddle up to her, she pulling me close. Thus we would sit for a while, holding and comforting each other. We had of course heard nothing from Pa, and we had received no word from Folkert and Frey since we left The Hague. Mail service was very, very slow and unreliable, if available at all. We also had to be careful; Mam could not address letters to Folkert for fear the Nazis would find out that he was staying in our house. She had sent a letter addressed to Frey and told her about our whereabouts, but so far we had received no reply. Also, neither they nor we had access to a telephone, so that type of communication was out of the question. In any event, as far as I knew, telephones were not even in operation anymore, except perhaps for official Nazi business.

Shortly after we had one of these talks, Mam would snap out of her sorrow and change the subject or say, "That's enough of that. We must look to the future. Everything will be all right. I'm sure our problems will be over soon. Before you know it we will all be together again and then this will be history. So let's get ready for bed and go to sleep. Tomorrow will be a better day." But I suspected that she was just trying to comfort me. Her thoughts were still with the uncertainty of my brother's freedom and what had become of my father.

One night, after the latest report about the Allies' advancement, Mam tossed and turned, obviously troubled about our situation. In the morning, as we were getting dressed, she said, "I think we should move on. Yesterday I talked to an officer of the Marechaussee who came to buy some cheese. I asked him if he knew my niece and her husband. He said that he did not know Pia but had at one time met Sjaak. He also told me that he had heard that Sjaak was no longer in Heerenveen, that he had been transferred to Joure. He believes that most likely that's where they now live. Joure is not far from here, and I think we should go and check it out. Perhaps Sjaak, being in the Marechaussee, can find out what is happening with Folkert and Frey. Perhaps he can get a message to them. Also, with the Allied forces now being so close, the war should be over soon and maybe, when the Germans are gone, he can help us get back to The Hague."

I listened to her words with mixed feelings. We had been on the farm a few months and I had grown to really like it there. I would sure miss the Hiemstras, especially Arie; and what about Bruin? I would really miss him. On the other hand, seeing Pia and Sjaak again sounded exciting too. I had spent a lot of time with them before the war, when my parents went on holidays. Pia was fourteen years older than I was, and when she was still single and living with her parents, Aunt Katrien and Uncle Henk, and dating Sjaak, I had come to know them both very well. The last time I had seen them was four years ago when they got married. Now they had three children, twins and a little baby.

Mam told the Hiemstras about her decision at the breakfast table. They were sad to see us go but understood Mam's reasoning. That day I said goodbye to the cows, the chickens, and my pal Bruin. Just before going to bed, I slipped out and once more had a cuddle with that wonderful horse. The next morning, our luggage heavy with a large cheese, butter, loaves of bread, and an extra bag with ready-to-eat sandwiches, we said goodbye to the Hiemstras and set off on the next leg of our trip.

17

We made good progress. We were well rested and, because of the work on the farm, in good physical condition. St. Nicolaasga was behind us and now we were heading northeast for Joure. It was still early in the morning, and chilly; our breath came out as steam. It was late February, and although the roads were clear, patches of snow could be seen in the fields. Frozen spots of ice glimmered in the early morning light. Far in the distance behind us we could hear faint sounds like thunder, caused by explosions that sometimes lit up the still darkish sky. The Canadian forces were advancing. Occasionally a German truck with soldiers overtook us, paying us no attention. I guessed they were fleeing from the front.

"Maybe we should go the other way," I said, "toward the Canadians. They are our friends, right?"

"Yes," Mam replied, "they are our friends, but no, we can't go to them because then we would have to go through the German lines first. The Germans would shoot us if we tried. Besides, even if they let us through, we would be in the middle of the fight. It's too dangerous. We might end up being killed in the crossfire."

I thought about Mam's reply. Of course it made sense. Yet somehow it seemed illogical to me to be moving away from the liberators when we wanted to be liberated.

Soon after our conversation we crossed paths with three men. One of them, a tall man in his thirties, said that they had tried to cross over to the advancing Allies but instead were almost captured by the Germans. Obviously, Mam had been right. The man also said that there was a lot of fierce fighting going on, causing destruction to roads, bridges, and buildings in many cities—some of which we had travelled through when we left The Hague.

"How do you know all this?" Mam asked.

"Oh, well..." He leaned toward Mam and whispered in her ear, "I have my sources." He straightened, looked around, and said, "We have to go." He gestured to the other men to follow him. They jumped over the roadside fence into the field on the other side and quickly disappeared.

"Hmm," said Mam. "Maybe they are with the Resistance."

We picked up our luggage and continued on our way. Except for more movement of German military vehicles, the rest of the walk was uneventful.

We arrived in Joure in the afternoon, having covered only a little over fifteen kilometres. At the beginning, our luggage hadn't seemed that heavy, but the load had become heavier and more cumbersome as time went on. When we entered Joure, we were exhausted—and we still had to go to the Marechaussee station to inquire about the whereabouts of Pia and Sjaak. Mam asked a passerby for directions, but he shook his head and said, "I don't know about the Marechaussee, but there's a police station in the Torenstraat. Perhaps that's what you're looking for." He pointed us in the right direction.

Fortunately, the station was only a short distance away. There was a constable sitting at a desk in the reception area. He looked us up and down, scrutinized our luggage, then asked Mam, "What brings you here?"

"We would like to know where we can find Officer Sjaak Batstra. He is with the Marechaussee," Mam replied. With a sigh of relief she put down her suitcase and the valise containing the heavy cheese. I had also put my stuff down, and I settled myself on Mam's suitcase.

"Sjaak Batstra?" the constable said. "Why are you looking for him?"

"I am his aunt," Mam said, "and we are visiting."

"Visiting. I see." He stroked his chin and again looked us over carefully. "Do you have some identification? May I please see your *stamkaart*?"

Mam opened her purse and handed him her identification card. "This is my son," she said, pointing at me.

The constable looked at Mam's *stamkaart* and then at me. "What is your name, son?" he asked, returning Mam's card to her.

"My name is Jan," I said, "and Sjaak and Pia are my cousins. We have come all the way from The Hague."

"Have you, now? That's a long way, all right." A smile appeared on the constable's face. "But," he said, turning to Mam, "I believe you are mistaken. There are no Marechaussee stationed here. They do come here on certain occasions, but they are based in Heerenveen."

"Oh, no!" Mam exclaimed. "How can that be? We were told by a Marechaussee officer in St. Nicolaasga that he was transferred here." Mam swayed dizzily, grabbing hold of the desk.

"Hold on," the constable said, getting up from his seat. "Let me get you a chair and see if we can sort this out." He left the reception area and went into one of the adjacent rooms. A moment later he came back with another officer, each of them carrying a chair. "This is Inspector Hoekstra," the constable said. Mam shook hands with the inspector and introduced me. The inspector gave me a friendly smile and positioned the chairs opposite the desk. "Here, sit down, both of you, and make yourselves comfortable," he said. "Would you like a cup of tea?"

"Yes, please," we both said eagerly.

The constable left and shortly thereafter returned with two cups of hot tea.

"Thank you very much," Mam said as she accepted her cup.

As we both sipped, the inspector sat down behind the desk and began turning the pages of a book that he had pulled from a filing cabinet.

"Batstra, Batstra," he mumbled as he turned the pages, scanning down the lines with the help of a thick forefinger. "Here it is," he suddenly exclaimed. "Sjaak Batstra, detachment Heerenveen." He closed the book and looked up. "Officer Batstra is still in Heerenveen."

"Thank goodness," Mam said with a sigh of relief. "At least he is still around. Well," she said to me, standing up and putting her teacup down, "we'd better get going. We have some more travelling to do."

"Wait a moment," the inspector said. "You two are not going anywhere tonight. You're both tired, and it's getting late. Besides, there is a curfew and you're not allowed out on the street after eight o'clock. Also, Heerenveen is still a long way to go. Just wait here and let me see what we can do."

He got up and went into one of the other rooms. We heard him talking to someone, and when he came back he said, "Come with me."

He grabbed our suitcases, Mam and I picked up our other bags, and we followed him down a corridor. Toward the middle of the corridor he opened a door and gestured us inside. "It is not a luxury hotel, but you can spend the night here." Pointing to another door in the corridor, he added, "The bathroom is over there."

In the room were two single beds and a sink. It was a room used by officers who were on night watch. Mam almost burst into tears as she thanked the inspector for his kindness and concern for our well-being. The inspector patted Mam consolingly on her shoulder.

"You make yourselves comfortable while I see if I can organize something for you to eat. You must be hungry." Then he turned around, left the room, and closed the door behind him.

"Well," Mam said, "I guess that's that. We stay here for the night and continue tomorrow morning." She sat down on one of the beds and patted the pillow. "Seems quite comfortable. Although we still have farther to go, at least we can rest in a safe place."

I sat down on the other bed and looked at my surroundings. It was quite bare and stark but much better than being under a bush at the roadside. I couldn't help thinking about our comfortable surroundings on the farm and my friends Arie and Bruin. What would tomorrow bring for us? I could tell that Mam was also deep in private thoughts. A knock on the door brought us both back to reality.

It was the inspector with the constable who had brought us the tea. They carried two big plates with steaming food. It was *zuurkool met spek*—sauerkraut with bacon—delicious! This was a typical Dutch dish. The sauerkraut is mixed with mashed potatoes, and the bacon is chopped into little squares and fried. Usually I liked to make a little indentation in the middle of the serving with my fork. That way I had a space for the bacon, which was added, sizzling hot, to the mixture already on the plate. To each forkful of sauerkraut I would add bacon bits by dipping it into the little pond.

"I have some good news," Inspector Hoekstra said as we dug in. "I have been able to contact Officer Batstra and we are trying to make arrangements to have you both brought to Heerenveen. But it won't be until tomorrow. I think we might be able to arrange some type of transport. He asked me to give you his best wishes and is looking forward to your arrival."

"Oh my, that is wonderful news," Mam said. "Again, thank you so much for allowing us to stay here and for looking after us."

"No problem," the inspector replied. "We have to look after our own—in this case, the aunt and cousin of a fellow officer." He gave me a wink.

Later that night, when snuggled down in bed, I remembered another thing the man we met on the road had told us. He had said that the people in the big cities (The Hague, Rotterdam, and Amsterdam) and in basically the entire western part of the Netherlands were so suffering from lack of food that thousands were dying. The situation was so bad that an agreement had been reached between the Allied forces, the Red Cross, and the Germans, allowing the British to drop food supplies from their planes in these areas. I wondered how my friends Dick, Tonny, and Wim were doing. Were they still alive? What about Folkert and Frey? Regardless of the good news about Sjaak Batstra I did not sleep well that night. I'd doze off for a little while only to wake up with worries about my friends and family. I had bad dreams that night too. I dreamt that I was paddling my *kano* with Dick and Tonny and suddenly saw them getting thinner and thinner until they turned into skeletons and then disappeared altogether. Yet the paddles kept on moving. I yelled at them, telling them to come back, but they didn't. Instead, a plane came roaring over and I could hear loud laughter coming from it. Maybe the nightmare sounds silly now—but at the time it was terrifying.

I think Mam didn't sleep too well that night, either. We were both drowsy and tired when we got up at about six o'clock the next morning. It was still dark and we sat on the edge of our beds for a while, waiting for the morning light to peek through the window. We washed our faces and brushed our teeth in the sink, then slowly got dressed. About an hour later, we spotted a hint of dawn in the sky.

A knock on the door produced a constable we hadn't met before. He introduced himself and said that the inspector was off duty and had gone home. He would be returning shortly. In the meantime, were we ready for some breakfast? We followed the constable to a small room that turned out to be a sort of combination kitchen and eating area. Two other constables were in the room. One was preparing something on the stove.

"Welcome," one of the constables said. "Sit down at the table and have some breakfast." Plates with bread, bacon, and eggs were put in front of us. Before we had finished our plates, Inspector Hoekstra walked in.

"Good morning," he said, sitting down next to Mam. "I hope you had a good sleep."

"Yes, thank you," Mam said. "Your hospitality is much appreciated. Everyone is so nice to us, and now this lovely breakfast. We don't know how to thank you all."

"Don't mention it," the inspector said. "We are glad to help." He took a sip from the cup of coffee that had been handed him. "Now, as far as the move to Heerenveen is concerned, there's a coal truck coming from Heerenveen with a load for the gas factory here in Joure. When the driver has made his delivery he'll be returning to Heerenveen. On the way he'll stop by to pick you up." He looked at me and chuckled. "There you go, Jan, no more walking, and no more suitcases to carry." After taking another sip from his coffee cup he added, "The driver should be here in about an hour, so there is plenty of time to get ready." He looked at his watch, pushed his chair back, and stood up. "I have to go now. The other officers will help you if you need anything." Mam and I stood up too. He put his arms around both of us and said, "The best to both of you. Have a safe trip."

Mam wiped a tear from her face as he left. Then she started gathering the dishes. "No, no," said the constable who had prepared the breakfast.

"Please, let me," said Mam. "It's the least I can do. Come on, Jan, give me a hand. We are going to clean up and let the officers get on with their work."

18

The coal truck was a large and heavy vehicle with a dump box. The driver had stowed our belongings behind and under the seat in the cab where all three of us were sitting. He was a cheery fellow who, when he wasn't talking, whistled while he drove, tapping his fingers to the beat of his tune on the steering wheel.

"It will take us only about twenty minutes to get there," he said, interrupting the song he was whistling. "Don't normally deliver coal to the gas factory here in Joure. It usually comes in by barge. They must have been running low and needed some in a hurry. Thought they had already closed down, but I guess they still operate occasionally. It's only a matter of time and they'll be closed permanently. We're running out of coal." For a moment he returned to whistling. Then he continued, "No traffic on the roads these days except for German tanks and troop trucks. Then there's the odd horse-drawn wagon and quite a few pedestrians, some of them pushing carts: people on the move, away from the large cities in the western provinces." He took a sideways glance at us. "I guess that's where you two are from as well."

"Yes," said Mam, "we came from The Hague. We stayed on a farm in St. Nicolaasga for a while and now, hopefully, we will be arriving at our final destination."

"Wow, The Hague. That's a long way. Did you come by train or car?"

"Some of it by train, but most of it was by walking."

He gave a big whistle. "Walking? That's amazing—must have taken a long time."

"Yes," Mam nodded, "it took forever."

"The trouble is, there are hardly any cars or trucks around anymore, most of them seized by the Germans. The only reason I still have this truck and am allowed to drive it is because they need coal to make gas for heat and cooking. But I don't know for how much longer because, as I said before, we are running out of coal. Most of the big cities in the south and west have been without gas and electricity for quite some time now. But then, who knows, the liberators are coming and soon it will all be over. They are getting pretty close. It's making the Germans nervous—" He broke off suddenly and said, "Hold on, what's that?"

Ahead of us, near a turn in the road, we saw what had startled the driver. Parked by the side of the pavement was a motorcycle with a sidecar. Three Germans, two wearing helmets, the third wearing an officer's cap, stood by the motorcycle. The two soldiers were carrying rifles; the officer wore a pistol in his belt. As we came nearer, he walked to the middle of the road and signalled to us to stop.

"What the…," mumbled the driver as he stepped on the brakes and brought the truck to a stop.

Mam grabbed my hand and held her breath as the officer opened the door on the driver's side. The two soldiers walked around the truck and looked in the empty box.

"*Papiere!*" the officer said to the driver.

The driver pulled his identification card from his jacket pocket and gave it to the officer. As the man looked at the card he looked at Mam and me.

"*Aussteigen,*" he said.

All three of us did as we were told and got out of the truck. The officer climbed into the cab as we stood by the roadside, the soldiers standing close by and watching us. The officer poked around in the vehicle and then came out, shutting the door behind him.

He walked around the truck looking for whatever he was looking for, climbed onto one of the rear wheels to look into the empty box, and then came over to us.

He said something to the driver in German, something neither he nor I could understand.

"He wants to know what you're hauling, where you have been, and where you are going," Mam translated for him.

"Coal," the driver said, "for Joure, for gas; to the factory."

Again the officer said something in German. This time Mam answered. Pointing at me she said, "This is my son. The driver is giving us a ride to Heerenveen, where he lives."

The German walked around us, slowly examining us up and down. Then he clicked his heels and motioned us back into the truck. Quickly we climbed back in. The driver started the engine, put the truck into gear, and let out the clutch. Off we went.

"Wow," the driver said, "that was a close call. I thought they were going to take my truck."

"Yes," Mam said, "I thought so too, but maybe they are checking for weapons or something, now that the Allies are coming so close."

"Yeah, who knows. Anyhow, I'm glad it's over and we are back on the road again...with my truck!" He started whistling a happy tune, his fingers tapping the steering wheel.

Soon the truck rolled into the city of Heerenveen. "Here we are," the driver said, pointing to a building, "the Marechaussee station. That's the end of your trip."

The truck came to a halt and we stepped out of the cab. The driver grabbed our luggage and put it on the sidewalk. Just then, the main door of the building opened and there stood Sjaak Batstra, a big smile on his face.

"Welcome to Heerenveen," he said, embracing both Mam and me. "Come, let's get you inside." He thanked the driver for his good deed, grabbed our belongings, and carried them inside.

Mam and I also thanked the driver and stood at the building's entrance, waving goodbye. We could see him whistling and tapping the steering wheel as the truck drove off.

As soon as we entered the building another surprise awaited us. "Pia, Pia!" I shouted and wrapped my arms around her. Mam was also excited and gave her a warm embrace.

"Where are the kids?" Mam asked.

"They are at home; our neighbour is watching them. I heard from Sjaak that you were arriving today and wanted to be here when you arrived. You are a bit late. What happened? We were getting worried."

Mam told them about our encounter with the German patrol which had delayed us for nearly an hour.

"Well," said Sjaak, who had listened closely to Mam's account of the incident, "it's good to see you both safe and sound. Let's go home where we can all relax."

Sjaak and Pia lived only a short distance from the station. We walked, Sjaak carrying the suitcases, Pia carrying the heavy cheese, Mam and I carrying the rest. About twenty minutes later we arrived at their home, which was a semi-detached house in a nice neighbourhood. The twin girls, Mieke and Tanja, were playing in the living room with their dolls. Their little brother, Freddy, was busy in a playpen. A nice lady with blond hair shook our hands as Pia introduced us. "And this is Marie, our neighbour who so kindly offered to look after this lot while I was gone."

The neighbour went back to her home in the other half of the duplex. Sjaak took us upstairs to a bedroom which was to be ours during our stay in Heerenveen. Mam unpacked our suitcases and got us settled in our new surroundings. In the bedroom were two single beds, and the bathroom was next door in the upstairs hallway. It looked as though we were going to be quite comfortable. The two girls were in another bedroom upstairs and Pia and Sjaak shared their bedroom, also upstairs, with the baby, who slept in a little cradle in a corner of their room.

Sjaak usually left for work early in the morning and returned just before dinnertime. Pia looked after the kids and Mam did most of the cooking. Food was scarce here, too, but we managed much better than in The Hague. The cheese we brought from the farm was savoured by all of us. When Mam and Pia were busy and Sjaak was away at work, I explored the neighbourhood. A few houses down the road I met a boy my age. His name was Koos. His father had been taken by the Germans and transported to a labour camp. Like me, he didn't know if he would ever see his father again. Our common situation made us instant friends. Through Koos I met some other kids. We played soccer and my favourite game, marbles. They had lots of spare time, since here in Heerenveen, also, most schools were closed.

In the evening, when Sjaak was home, we played board games. Sometimes Koos joined us. There was sporadic electricity here, which came from the main electrical plant in the city of Leeuwarden. It would go on for a little while and then suddenly go off. If the power went off, we'd light some candles or an oil lamp. Those evenings were fun.

Sjaak had an extraordinary talent for killing flies. His way of shooting them with his thumb and forefinger fascinated me. He would bend and press the tip of his forefinger against his thumb and slowly move to where the fly was sitting. Then, snap! The fly was hit and fell to the floor. I tried it too, but the fly always got away before I snapped my finger, or I would snap it but the fly would just fly away unharmed. "The secret," Sjaak said, "is that you must approach him from behind so that he can't see you. Like so..." He would do it again and the fly would drop to the floor. No matter how hard I tried, I could not do it. Sjaak could even get a fly when it was still flying. He followed it as it flew around until...snap. There, he got it again! It was truly amazing. If he was as good at catching criminals as he was at catching flies, he definitely would have been a valued member of the Marechaussee.

Since the invasion, the Marechaussee had been placed under the command and scrutiny of the German authorities. Before the war they were called the Royal Marechaussee and were a military police force. Now they were simply called Marechaussee and served as a regular policing authority. Their resources were limited but they still had connections and ways of obtaining information. After some inquiries, Sjaak was able to find something out about Folkert and Frey. According to Sjaak's informant, they were both alive and well. Mam and I breathed a huge sigh of relief when Sjaak gave us the good news.

19

The liberators' advance toward Heerenveen became more and more the talk of the day. Everyone knew that the Allies were making good progress and the day of liberation was close. Then, all of a sudden—I believe it was on April 14, 1945—tanks, jeeps, and trucks followed by marching soldiers arrived in the city. They were Canadians! Large cheering crowds lined the streets. People were waving, shouting, and throwing confetti and flowers from the windows of the buildings located along the route. The red, white, and blue flag of Holland and flags of the House of Orange flapped in the wind. People climbed onto the tanks and jumped onto the jeeps and trucks, embracing the soldiers. Soon, the marching soldiers were accompanied by hordes of civilians, children, women, and men, all ecstatic with the arrival of these heroes. What a day! Fires were lit in the middle of streets and squares; people danced and celebrated. As we joined in, Mam cried with joy, tears running down her cheeks. "Soon, all will be back to normal," she told me. "All we need now is to hear from Pa and have him come home again."

Koos and I joined a bunch of other kids following the soldiers to the park where they set up camp. They showed us their guns and inside the tanks and gave us chocolate bars. For several days, right after breakfast, we went to the park and hung around there for the rest of the day. The place was busy. People came with their antique clocks, Delft Blue vases, and other Dutch curios and

A Canadian army truck welcomed by a jubilant crowd during the Dutch liberation, 1945 (photographer unknown).

traded with the soldiers for cigarettes, loaves of bread, and canned food. One man even dragged over an old wood-burning stove.

Many friendships were struck, and some soldiers started dating Dutch girls. Such things were happening all over the country, wherever the liberating forces were stationed. Plenty of these relationships resulted in weddings. My own cousin Corry, who lived in Bussum, a city in the province of North Holland, fell in love with a Canadian soldier and became one of many Canadian war brides. She and her husband, John Kriticos, started a restaurant in Montreal.

One thing we noticed was that the Canadians were very relaxed in their methods. We were used to the German way of doing things: the shouting of commands, the obeying of orders accompanied by the clicking of boots; discipline! The Canadians tolerated all the goings-on in the park, kids playing and local people hanging around trading goods. Every once in a while, a couple of soldiers would walk over to a cannon, put ammunition in it, and fire it off in the direction where battles were still being fought—toward Leeuwarden, a larger city to the north of us that was still in German hands. Then they would calmly walk back to whomever they had been chatting with.

One day, Mam, Pia, and I were walking through the town when we noticed a large crowd. When we went to see what was going on, we saw several men who had dragged young women to the area where the crowd was gathered. The men wore armbands on their upper coat sleeves. The letters BS were marked on them—Binnenlandse Strijdkrachten, or the Homeland Militia.

"Who are those men and what are they doing with those girls?" Mam wondered.

"Those fellows are part of the Dutch Resistance," said Pia. "What they are doing with those girls, I don't know."

We soon found out. The women, most of whom were in their late teens or early twenties, had been accused of dating German soldiers. They were to be the objects of a public demonstration showing how German sympathizers were to be dealt with. One by one, the girls were dragged to the centre of the crowd, where, held firmly by two of the Resistance men, a third man proceeded to shave them bald. The girls were crying and in obvious despair.

"This is terrible," Mam said. "Don't those men have better things to do than humiliate those defenceless girls?"

Many of the crowd were cheering, but I noticed others who, like Mam and Pia, watched with disapproval.

"I can't look at this anymore," Mam said. "Let's get away from here."

Pia agreed and we left.

As we walked away from the scene, Mam said to Pia, "Who knows why those girls dated German soldiers—maybe it supplied them with some food. In any event, if capturing those girls and humiliating them is a demonstration of the heroism of the Dutch Resistance, then I'm sorry, but I can't be very proud of those so-called heroes. Where were they when the Germans were still here? Did they do anything worthwhile then?"

"Who knows?" said Pia. "Now that the war is over, Resistance fighters seem to crawl out of the woodwork everywhere. Obviously, many are fakes—they were nowhere to be seen when they were really needed, and now they go around showing their authority and putting on these 'demonstrations.' They disrupt the order the police force is trying to maintain."

I listened to this conversation with interest. I was reminded of the time Pa had turned down an invitation to join the Resistance. What we had just witnessed seemed to prove what he had said: many of those freedom fighters could not be trusted and were in it only to boost their own ego and brag about it to others. I was sure that those men who had really made a difference, who had put their lives on the line, wouldn't want to be involved in anything as cowardly as this.

That evening, when seated around the table in Pia and Sjaak's living room, we told Sjaak about what we had seen.

"Yes," said Sjaak. "There is a lot of that going on. Even among the fellows who really belonged to the Resistance there were some idiots who caused nothing but problems. On the other hand, there were many times when the Dutch Resistance was a force to be reckoned with. The attack on a prison in Leeuwarden that allowed forty political prisoners to escape; the passing of valuable information to the Allies...Resistance fighters often really helped the cause."

Sjaak paused and started to turn a page of the book he was reading. I was eager for him to go on and asked, "So what were some of the problems they created?"

Sjaak put down his book. "Well," he began, "a lot of the information they passed on to the Allies was incorrect or unreliable. The Allies were aware of this, and sometimes correct information was not acted upon because they were uncertain of its reliability. And you've heard about the massacre in Putten, haven't you?"

"Yes," I answered. "I suppose everybody has. Many people arrested and houses burned. But the Germans did that. What does it have to do with the Dutch Resistance?"

"Well, I'll tell you. I read a report on it, earlier today."

I noticed Pia and Mam also leaning in to listen to what Sjaak had to say.

"You must understand that the Resistance was a rather fragmented organization consisting of small groups in various areas, working independently. Often, one group didn't know what another group was doing. One fellow who should not have been in the Resistance was in command of such a group—a man named Witvoet. He believed that important documents were in the hands of a German patrol on its way to Putten. He took his men to the Oldenallerbrug, a bridge on the route, where he set up a machine gun. But when the machine gun operator settled himself behind the weapon, he saw that it would not be able to cover the area through which the German patrol was expected to travel. When he and his comrades searched for their commander to query him about the gun's position, they found Witvoet hiding at a farm across the street, shivering with fright."

"No kidding," I exclaimed. "Some commander!"

"Unbelievable," Mam said, shaking her head. Pia also shook her head in disgust.

"Anyhow," Sjaak continued, "the men persuaded the hero to leave his hiding place and the machine gun was moved to the top of the cab of a truck that was parked near the bridge. Shortly after the men had taken up their positions, the Germans started to arrive. Lights were turned on to blind them, and the machine gun trigger was pulled. But the thing would not fire."

"Another blunder," Pia commented.

"Yes," said Sjaak. "Isn't that something? The Germans had started to fire immediately when the lights were turned on. When one of the German vehicles had nearly passed, the Dutch machine gun finally started firing. The German car was struck and drove off the road. Commander Witvoet panicked and ran away, but was called back by one of his men. Then a second German vehicle arrived. After a few more shots were fired, again, Witvoet ran away from the scene, and this time he did not return."

"What a coward," I said.

"Yes," said Sjaak. "It's not the behaviour you'd expect from a leader."

While Sjaak was talking, Pia had made some "ersatz coffee," the surrogate brew of mainly chicory that people were drinking since real coffee had become unavailable. "Thanks," said Sjaak, as Pia put a cup in front of him. He took a sip and continued his report of the event.

"A German officer was lying on the ground by the struck car. He had been shot in the knee. Another German officer was shot in the stomach. The officer with the knee wound was searched and found to be carrying a map with part of Hitler's headquarters. He was put into the truck together with Frans Slotboom, one of the Resistance men, who had also been shot in the stomach.

The Resistance fighters drove the truck to their hiding place in the forest. Frans did not survive his injuries and was buried by his mates in the forest."

"How awful," Pia commented.

"Yes. In the meantime," Sjaak added, "the other wounded officer had escaped with two junior officers."

"All this took place on the night of September 30, 1944. Early in the morning of the following Sunday, Putten was surrounded. Anyone found in the vicinity of the bridge was arrested and held in a nearby meadow. Many of these people were innocent passersby: people in search of food, and farmers on their way to milk their cows. Of these people, eight, including a young woman who tried to run away, were shot right there by the Germans who held them captive."

"What a horror story!" Mam interrupted.

"But that was only the beginning," said Sjaak. "The entire population of Putten knew that repercussions were sure to follow, and that all the men, but especially those between the ages of eighteen and fifty, were at great risk. But before they even had time to hide them, at nine o'clock in the morning of that dreadful day, the order came from General Christiansen, the German High Command of the Netherlands, to arrest everybody in the village except those who were known to be pro-German. The women and children were confined in a church. The men were gathered on a school field behind the church. Thirty of these men were lined up against the wall, with a corpse in front of them. In the meantime, houses were being searched, and anyone hiding rounded up."

Sjaak finished his coffee, put down the cup, and said, "Well, you know what happened. The next morning all the men were moved to the market square, a detachment of German soldiers standing by, ready to fire. The German commander told them that if anyone had information about the Resistance attack that would lead to the arrest of the culprits, he would be able to rescind the orders he had been given. Nobody came forward. So the orders were carried out: those belonging to the NSB and others who worked for the Germans were allowed to leave; the remaining men, some six hundred of them, were taken to the railroad station to be transported to labour camps in Germany. The other inhabitants, women and children, were given three hours to leave the village. After that, 105 houses were set on fire."

There was dead silence when Sjaak finished. The impact of hearing the whole story was hard to take.

Sjaak broke the silence. "We've now learned that the captured German officer had actually been let go by the Resistance group. And the map, that important document, turned out to be of little value to the Allied forces."

"So the whole thing was for nothing," Mam remarked sadly. "All this misery, the killing, the burning of houses, those men transported to Germany: all for a piece of paper that turned out to be useless."

"How did you find out all those details?" Pia asked.

"There is a warrant for the arrest of Witvoet," Sjaak answered. "It came with a full report about the whole incident."

Much later, we learned that of the six hundred men who ended up in German labour camps, only forty survived.

20

With the Germans gone, we listened to the BBC constantly, anxiously awaiting news about the fronts and the progress of the liberation. The western provinces were still to be liberated; the northern part of Friesland and part of the province of Groningen were also still under German occupation. Finally, on May 5, 1945, the Germans capitulated and Holland was officially free. But the trouble wasn't over yet. In the larger cities, the Allies had not yet taken control. On May 7, German marines started shooting in Amsterdam, killing twenty-two people and injuring well over a hundred. On May 8, Allied troops moved into the city and Amsterdamers could relax. Schiermonnikoog, an island in the north, had to wait until June 12 before it was cleared of the Nazis.

Mam wanted to go back to The Hague as soon as possible. I did too. I wanted to see my brother and my father. Sjaak kept telling us to wait. "It's not safe yet," he would say. "You have to wait until the whole country has been cleared of Nazi activity."

Every night, before going to sleep, Mam and I talked about our much anticipated return home.

"How do we go back, Mam?" I asked one night. "There are still no trains or buses. Do we have to walk again?"

"I don't know," said Mam. "We'll deal with that when we come to it."

I had befriended two soldiers whom I regularly went to see in the park. They couldn't speak Dutch and I couldn't speak much English, though I was learning pretty quickly. I could say yes and no, and they taught me to count. I also picked up expressions such as "holy cow" and some others that I was told not to repeat when in the company of my mother. One way or another, we were able to communicate pretty well. Several times I brought them home to meet Mam, Pia, Sjaak, and the kids. They were really nice guys and every time they came over they brought chocolate bars and loaves of bread. The bread they brought was delicious. It was very white. I had never seen or tasted such white bread—it tasted like cake.

Often when I saw them I talked to them about our wish to go back to The Hague. One day, when the two soldiers were visiting with us again, they told us that they could probably arrange for us to be taken to Zwolle. One of their mates was a courier who travelled regularly by jeep between different command posts. They had also heard that the milk processing plant in Zwolle drove trucks with milk to the cities in the western provinces and that they took passengers, dislocated people such as us, along on their routes. With great excitement Mam discussed this opportunity with Sjaak, who after a few inquiries confirmed that, indeed, the processing plant was helping people to get back to their home cities.

With the help of my soldier friends it was arranged that we would get a ride to Zwolle.

The fellow who gave us the ride was a corporal named Herbert Lund. He told us that his grandparents had been Swedish immigrants. "Call me Herb," he said.

"Hello, Herb," Mam said. In broken English, she introduced herself and me and expressed her appreciation for the lift.

His jeep was parked in front of the house. The two soldiers were there too, to wish us a good journey. Pia, Sjaak, and the kids had gathered around the jeep as we shook hands, embraced, and kissed farewell. It was quite an emotional occasion. Mam and

Herbert Lund, the Canadian soldier who drove us to Zwolle, 1945.

Pia hugged for a long time. I had a lump in my throat and was close to tears now that the final moment had come. But I was also excited—we were going home! Home to my brother and Frey, and my friends in The Hague. I expected to see my father again soon too.

Sjaak put our luggage in the back of the jeep. I sat beside it and Mam sat in the front with Herb.

Herb started the engine and drove off, sounding the horn. I stood up and waved to the group behind us until we turned a corner and lost sight of them. Then I settled down in my seat and began looking around. Next to me, in the right rear corner of the vehicle, was a large metal thing firmly bolted down. It had knobs and dials on it and a long metal stick extending upwards from it that looked like a fishing rod. Later Herb told me that the rod was an antenna and the metal box a two-way radio with which he could contact the command post. "Wow," I thought, "this is like the crystal receivers I built, but it's a transmitter as well—the real thing!"

The wind blew into our faces as we drove along the roads. The jeep's top was down and there were no side windows. The weather was nice, a June day with lots of sunshine, only a few clouds in the sky. Herb handled the vehicle expertly while chatting with Mam. I was enjoying every minute of the trip. The countryside was beautiful. Cows were in the fields; buttercups were blooming. People waved at us as we passed. I couldn't stop thinking about Folkert and Frey. Soon we would be together again. We hadn't heard from Pa for a long time, but I was certain he must be on his way home. Maybe he was already there! Soon I would see them all again. I cheerfully waved at the driver of a horse-drawn wagon when we overtook him. The man nodded his head and lifted his whip in salute.

We reached Zwolle in the middle of the afternoon. Herb drove us straight to the processing plant. There was a large crowd of people near the front entrance. Some were sitting on the grass;

others were standing, chatting with one another. All of them had suitcases, knapsacks, and other luggage.

"Holy cow," I said to Herb, showing off my knowledge of the English language as we pulled up in front of the building. "Many." I pointed to the crowd.

Herb laughed and slapped me on the shoulder. "You're learning fast," he chuckled.

We took our luggage from the jeep and said goodbye to Herb. "Thank you, Herb," Mam said in English, kissing him on both cheeks. "We not forget this." We both waved as he drove off.

We passed the waiting people and entered the building. More people were inside, in a large reception area. They were sitting on benches and chairs, luggage spread around them. At the rear of the large room was a man who looked official; he had a clipboard in his hand and was writing on it while a woman with two children talked.

"Let's go over there," Mam said. "That must be the person we need to see." Just as we approached, the woman and her two children moved to a vacant bench to sit down.

"Hello," said Mam. "Are you the person who can get us a ride home?"

The man looked up from his clipboard. "Yes," he said, "depending on where you want to go."

"The Hague," Mam answered.

"Ah, The Hague! Most are going to Amsterdam. Just the two of you?" He looked at Mam and me.

"Yes," Mam said, "just the two of us."

"Well, let's see." He looked at his clipboard and turned some of the pages attached to it. "You're in luck! I can get you a ride tomorrow. How is that?"

"Fabulous," Mam answered excitedly.

"Okay, then, let's get that organized. What are your names?"

Mam gave him the information. The man wrote it down and said, "The truck leaves at six in the morning, and to be on the safe side, you'd better be here by half past five. If you're not here on time, the truck will leave without you."

"Oh, we'll be here on time, don't you worry!" Mam assured him.

"Good. In the meantime, you can stay here. We have no overnight accommodation, but you're welcome to find yourself a seat in the reception area, or outside, whichever you prefer."

"Thank you very much," we both said. Then Mam suggested to me, "Let's go outside. It's a nice day; we might as well enjoy it."

Most of the grassy patches outside were occupied by other people. Mam stood still and looked around, then suddenly made a decision. "We have until tomorrow morning," she said. "That leaves us lots of time. I don't feel like hanging around here, so why don't we go down the road and see what else is around? What do you think, Jan?"

Mam didn't wait for my answer. She picked up her share of the luggage and I picked up mine. We walked back onto the road where we stopped, looking left and right.

"Look, Mam," I said. "Over there, where those trees are."

"Yes," said Mam, "I see it. Looks like a peaceful area. Let's walk in that direction. We can have a little picnic there, and maybe find a place to spend the night." We had with us a bag of sandwiches and other goodies that had been given to us by my soldier friends.

We didn't have far to walk. The treed area bordered a farm, and as we were eating our sandwiches, we spotted a haystack. It was situated alongside the path that was the main entrance to the farm.

"That would be a good place to spend the night," I said.

"Yes," said Mam. "We can't just go in there, though. For one thing, I don't see a ladder, and in any event, it would be better if we asked the farmer for permission."

I was determined not to let this chance go by. I liked sleeping in haystacks—it was soft, warm, and cozy. "It's only about one metre high. We can easily sneak in there without being noticed," I pointed out.

"You are a naughty boy," Mam laughed. "What if he sees us when we're climbing in—or comes to get some hay and finds us? No, I think we should ask for permission. We've only been refused that once. Remember? Along the dike of the IJssel? That farmer said that he did not want his hay contaminated by city slobs."

I remembered that all too well. The fellow was a real nasty old cuss, probably a friend of the Nazis. We had had better luck with his neighbour, who received us with much kindness.

"Have you finished your sandwich?" Mam asked. "Don't start on the chocolate bars; we'll save them for later. Let's go."

We stood up, gathered our gear, and proceeded along the path toward the farm. We passed the haystack and came to a side entrance of the farmhouse. Almost as soon as Mam had knocked, the door opened, and a woman looked at us questioningly.

"We are from The Hague, and we are getting a ride with one of the milk trucks from the dairy factory. The truck is not leaving until tomorrow morning, and I wonder if my son and I could spend the night in your haystack."

A big smile appeared on the woman's face. "Sure, go ahead. I would let you sleep in a bed if I had one available, but I don't."

"Oh, no, that's not necessary; we'll be quite comfortable in the haystack. We don't want to put you to any trouble," Mam added hastily.

"Oh, no trouble. It's still too early to go to sleep—why don't you come in? I was just about to make a cup of tea." She opened the door wide and we entered the home.

"That's very kind of you," Mam said.

"Don't mention it; I can use the company. My husband and sons are at the market in town and won't be back for some time." The woman chatted while she was busy at the stove where a large kettle sat blowing off steam. "Would you like a sandwich?"

"No, thank you. We just had something to eat."

"How about a piece of cake, then? Fresh from the oven." She put on a glove and pulled a baking tin out of the oven. A delicious aroma immediately spread through the kitchen where we had sat ourselves down at the table. She flipped the tin on a wooden board and out came a beautiful cake. "It needs to cool off a little bit before I can cut it, but we have lots of time. Here," she said, pouring the boiling water onto the tea in the teapot, "help yourself to a cup." She put the pot on the table where the cups and saucers were already waiting and sat down opposite Mam.

"This won't be the first time we've had people sleeping in our haystack," the woman said. "Before the liberation, especially last winter, people crawled in there all the time. I can't remember how often we went to get hay and found people curled up inside. We didn't mind—we left a ladder against it so that people could get to the top and get in without spilling hay on the ground."

We chatted some more and then she said, "Let's see if that cake has cooled enough." She stood up, touched the cake carefully, and then began slicing it. "There we are," she said with a satisfied smile on her face, putting a large plate loaded with cake slices on the table. "Help yourself. Take as many as you like. They are still a little bit hot so don't get burned." She put a dish of whipped cream on the table beside the cake.

I couldn't wait. I grabbed a slice of cake and put lots of whipped cream on it. Mmm, delicious! While Mam and the lady were talking I gobbled down my slice, and was about to grab another one when Mam stopped me. "Hey, young man, don't be so greedy! You just had sandwiches, then tea, and now cake... take a break, give your tummy a rest, and watch your manners." I quickly pulled my hand away from the cake dish and, somewhat embarrassed, leaned back in my chair.

"I'm glad that you like my cake so much," laughed the lady. "How would it be if I wrap up some slices for you to take with you?" I wasn't going to argue with that.

While Mam and the lady kept chatting, I excused myself and went for a look around the farm. I felt comfortable there; it reminded me of the Hiemstras'. With a professional eye I looked at the chicken coop and saw that it had been cleaned recently. It was open and the chickens wandered through the farmyard. I said hello to a few hens that were following me around, expecting to get fed. I found a bit of grain and threw it onto the ground. Soon, other chickens ran toward the spot and with a lot of cackling started picking up the food. Behind a big barn I spotted a horse, a big fellow with black and white markings and huge feet. Perhaps a cross between a Gelderlander and a Friesian, I thought. He turned out to be a friendly guy who came toward me as soon as I approached the fence surrounding his paddock. Standing on one of the boards of the fence, I patted him. He responded with an affectionate snort and then started to nuzzle the sleeve of my jacket. His manners reminded me of Bruin. I wondered how my old pal was doing. And did Arie need to cut more willow trees for his supply of wooden shoes?

While stroking the horse, I looked around me. The whole place gave me a really good feeling. Maybe I should become a farmer someday, I thought.

My daydream was interrupted by Mam's call. "I have to go now," I said to the horse, giving him a few more rubs on his forehead. Somewhat reluctantly, I lowered myself off the fence and went back to the farmhouse.

Mam stood waiting there. "Come on," she said. "Let's go."

We walked around the area until Mam said, "We have to get up really early tomorrow morning, so we might as well get some rest."

We had left our suitcases at the farm, to be fetched tomorrow. The farmer's wife had said that she would leave the door open so that we could get them in case the family was still asleep. A short ladder stood by the haystack. We climbed it and made ourselves comfortable in the soft hay. A few minutes after we had lain down we saw a swallow flying over our heads. Then we noticed a nest stuffed away in the rafters in the peak of the roof, almost directly above us. It was full of young ones. The parent swallow fed them and then flew away. A few moments later it returned with another savoury morsel. Each time, as soon as the parent bird arrived, wide open, little yellow beaks popped up above the nest, and as soon as the bird flew out to fetch more food, they disappeared.

"This is a good sign," Mam said, whispering so as not to frighten the small creatures.

"Is it, Mam?" I asked, keeping my voice down.

"Yes," she said softly. "It's a sign of spring, of new life, of better things to come."

I snuggled up to her and dozed off into a comfortable sleep.

The next morning we arrived at the dairy factory a few minutes after five. A big tank truck was parked in front of the building, surrounded by people.

"I wonder if that's our truck," I said.

Mam picked up her pace, then pushed her way through the crowd to the clipboard-holding man at the centre. I followed closely behind, a little breathless with the rush.

"Excuse me," Mam said in a loud voice, when she was close enough to be heard. "Is this the truck that is going to The Hague?"

The man looked up from his clipboard, searching over the heads of the people until he spotted Mam. "No, madam, this truck is going to Amsterdam. What is your name?"

Mam gave him her name and added, "And this is my son Jan."

The man stretched his neck but couldn't see me because the people around me were grown-ups much taller than I was. Giving up, he looked back at his clipboard and turned a few pages of the notebook attached to it. "Oh, yes, I have it right here. You will be on the truck that's leaving at six o'clock. It is presently being loaded and will be here soon. Just be patient and await your turn."

"Oh, thank you," said Mam. As we made our way out of the crowd, she said to me, "For a moment there, I was afraid that something had gone amiss and that we were too late."

"But Mam," I said, "we were told that our truck would be leaving at six, and it's not even five-thirty yet. How could we be too late?"

"Well, you never know. Sometimes plans change. I was afraid that our truck had been rescheduled to leave earlier."

I understood. Now that we were so close, it would have been terrible to miss this opportunity to get home.

We found a spot on the grass to sit and wait. It was wet from the early morning dew, but we didn't care. We were too excited about our forthcoming trip to The Hague.

In a short while the parked truck fired up. People climbed into the cab and onto the back alongside the tank. Some were even seated on top of it. Mam and I looked at the spectacle in awe.

"Oh dear," Mam said, "that looks dangerous to me. I hope we don't have to travel that way."

Suddenly the man with the clipboard ran toward the truck. "No, no, no," he yelled. "Get off! You can't sit on top of the tank. Only those people whom I have named are allowed on this truck. All the others please get off. You'll have to wait your turn." A few people reluctantly climbed off the truck, but others would not leave. "You have to get off," the man yelled again. "This truck will not leave until you do." He said something to the truck driver, and suddenly the engine was turned off. Now his words were taken seriously. More people descended from the truck. The man with the clipboard started calling names. "Brinkhof, van der Waard…" Each time he called a name it was answered with "Here." When the man had counted the passengers on the truck, he gave a signal to the driver. The engine was restarted and the truck drove off. Almost at the same time another truck appeared.

"This must be ours," Mam said. "Why don't you stay here while I go and find out." I watched her as she approached the man in charge. When she spoke, I saw him looking at his clipboard again and then nodding his head. Mam turned around and hurried back to me. "Yes, that's it," she called cheerfully, while still some distance away.

I started gathering our luggage.

"He said he would call us as soon as the truck is ready to leave," Mam said. "We are very, very lucky, because apparently we are still the only passengers going to The Hague. Everyone else is going to Amsterdam. He said to me that it changes from day to day; perhaps tomorrow there will be a bunch that has to go to Rotterdam or The Hague. Anyhow, this means we get to sit in the cab with the driver. Isn't that great?" Mam was beside herself with joy.

A short while later we boarded the truck.

21

I don't remember much about the trip. I was mesmerized by the constant drone of the engine, the speed at which the landscape flowed past us, and the anticipation of arriving in The Hague, seeing my friends, my brother. It was hard to imagine that the distance we had walked over so many long weeks would now be covered in less than a day. This very day we would be back at the home we had left...when? I dozed off, then woke up and heard Mam chatting with the driver. I dozed off again, half imagining, half dreaming about arriving at our house: embracing Frey and Folkert, seeing Dick, Tonny, and Wim, telling them about my adventures, finding out what had happened to them while I was gone. Suddenly the truck rolled into the outskirts of the city. I was wide awake now, watching the familiar buildings and streets pass by. My heart pounded. Almost there! The truck negotiated a few more streets and then came to a halt at the local dairy facility. We stepped out of the cab, collected our luggage, thanked the driver, and started walking.

We still had a fair distance to go but it seemed like nothing. We walked through the familiar streets, coming closer and closer. Now we were on the De La Rey weg, then on the bridge crossing the Laak. We wanted to run but couldn't because of the luggage we were carrying. Our hurrying was tiring us out too.

"I have to sit down and catch my breath for a minute," Mam said.

We sat down on our suitcases, both of us huffing and puffing. In the distance we could see the corner of the Hadewiech Straat and the Moerweg, our home. We could see the soccer fields, the Zuiderpark, and the Beek: all those familiar places. "Okay, let's go," Mam said, picking up her luggage. "Just a few more steps and we'll be there."

A short while later, we rang the bell and pounded on the door of number 168. The door opened and Folkert stood before us. He was soon joined by Frey. We hugged, we cried, we danced, we were overcome with joy. Sometimes we were all talking at the same time, trying to bring one another up to date on the things that had happened. Eventually we calmed down and listened to one another with full attention. One piece of bad news was about our sailboat. Shortly after we had left for Friesland, Folkert had gone to the mooring place to haul it out of the water and have it stored on land for the winter. When Folkert arrived at the farm all the boats had disappeared—including ours! When Folkert inquired at the farm, he was told that the boat had been taken by the Germans the week before.

"Taken by the Germans?" Folkert had asked. "Are you sure?"

"Oh, yes," said the farmer. "They knew exactly what they were looking for; they knew the name of the boat and the name of the owner, your father."

"Where did they take it?"

"No idea," the farmer replied. "I asked but they wouldn't tell me. They said it was being confiscated by the German Reich. I wasn't going to ask again, because they were not very friendly and told me that I could be in trouble for harbouring the possessions of an enemy of the Führer. They towed it away with a small motorboat. I would have told you, but I had no way of getting in touch with you."

We listened quietly to Folkert's account. "Well," Mam said after a moment of silence, "that's unfortunate, but at least you are both here and so are we. And that is the most important thing."

"Yes," Folkert agreed, "and the boat has to be somewhere, so maybe we can track it down and get it back."

"I hope so," I grumbled. I couldn't imagine life without our sailboat.

Mam soon asked the question that was pressing on our minds. "Have you heard from Pa?"

"No, not a thing," Folkert answered. "Have you?"

"No," said Mam. "I guess we'll have to wait. Hopefully, no news is good news."

"Yes," said Folkert. "Those concentration camps are a long way from here. It may take some time before he can get back. Even to get a message to us may be difficult. Everything is still in chaos."

It was late in the evening when we finally went to bed. We had arrived just before dusk. The hours had gone by quickly. I had wanted to go and see Dick and Tonny, but Mam wouldn't let me. "That will have to wait till tomorrow," she said. "It's too late; your friends must be sound asleep by now."

That night I slept in my own bed. It felt great! The day had turned out to be almost exactly as I had hoped. The big disappointment was not to have seen Pa. I'd fully expected him to be home, where he belonged.

The next morning I woke up early, put on my clothes, and sneaked out the front door. I went upstairs and rang the bell at Dick's apartment. It took a while before Mrs. van Duin, Dick's mother, opened the door. She was dressed in a housecoat and stared at me with surprise. "Jan, where did you come from?" She rubbed her eyes, wondering if she was seeing things.

"We came back yesterday. Yesterday evening. Mam is here too. She's still asleep. Is Dick home?"

"Yes, he is home but he's still in bed. What time is it?" She looked at the clock in the hallway. "Oh dear, it is just after six o'clock. You're a bit early, aren't you? Does your mother know you're here?"

"No, she doesn't. Everybody is still asleep."

"Well, I'm not surprised. I guess you're looking forward to seeing your friend." Then she smiled and said, "Come on in and I'll wake him up. I'm sure he is just as anxious to see you."

I stepped through the door and followed her inside. She entered Dick's room while I looked in. Dick was covered in blankets. Even his head was hidden under them. Mrs. van Duin pulled the cover from his face and touched his shoulders. "Look who's here," she said. Dick's eyes opened, his eyelids blinking against the morning light. He groaned as he turned around. Then he saw me standing by the door. At once he sat up straight. "Jan," he screamed, "you're back!" I ran toward him as he jumped out of bed. We grabbed each other's hands and started to dance in a circle. Laughing, Dick's mother watched our antics for a little while and then left the room.

Dick and I talked and talked. I told him about everything that had happened to us, about the attack on the train, about sleeping in haystacks, about the Hiemstra farm and all the other things that came to my mind at that moment. Every now and then Dick's mother joined us and listened to the conversation. We both had stories to tell; it would take days to catch up with all the news.

Mrs. van Duin came into the room again. "Dick," she said, "it's time to get dressed. Jan, you'd better go home now before your mother starts wondering where you are. Dick will join you later. I'll come too, to see your *moeder*."

"Okay," said Dick. "I'll be down at your place soon, and then we can go and see Tonny."

"Yeah," I said, "that's a good idea. He should be awake by now."

I left Dick's place and went home. Mam had just got up. She and Frey were chatting at the kitchen table. I told her I had gone to see Dick and that he and his mother would be dropping by soon. "Oh, that's great," Mam said. "It'll be good to see her." Mam and Mrs. van Duin were good friends. "Here, would you like some biscuits?" She proffered a plate. I took one and after a few bites I said, "Mmm, those are good. Where did they come from?"

"From the Red Cross and the Allies," Frey replied. "They come in these. Look." She produced a large tin about forty by forty centimetres at the square ends, and about eighty centimetres high. The corners were slightly rounded. At the top was a circular lid that pressed down into an opening at the top. "They were dropped from the planes by parachute," Frey said. She put the tin back on the floor in a corner of the kitchen with several others. "Now they're brought in by trucks. They helped us survive, though for many they came too late. Even now, if it wasn't for this emergency food we would still be very hungry." Smoothing her blouse, she turned to Mam and added, "The parachutes came in handy too. I made this blouse from the fabric. I have lots of this cloth left over and I can make you a blouse too."

I wasn't too interested in the clothes possibilities, but I looked thoughtfully at the large tins. I remembered seeing some in the hallway of Dick's apartment, and also in the portico when I went up the stairs.

Then Dick and his mother arrived, and Dick and I left the women chatting while we went to Tonny's apartment. We were greeted with the same surprised and happy welcome. After we had talked and reminisced for a while, I pointed at the biscuit tins stored in Tonny's hallway. "More biscuit tins," I said. "Dick has tins; we have tins—how many of those tins are there?" I asked.

"Those? Hundreds, probably thousands. They're stashed away everywhere," my friends answered. "Why?"

"I don't know, but it seems to me they could be used for something."

"Like what?"

"A boat," I said. "I bet those tins are watertight. If we have enough of them and somehow tie them together we should be able to make a platform large enough to sit on and stay afloat. I wish I had paid better attention to that thing I saw yesterday—a sort of raft that a boy was paddling on the Laak. It was really bright and shiny—I'm pretty sure it was made of biscuit tins."

Tonny and Dick looked at each other. Then Dick said, "Okay, you got us. Let's give it a try—sounds like fun."

22

While we worked on our biscuit-tin boat, Dick and Tonny told me how tough things had been during the past winter. They had barely managed to survive. Some of the apartments were empty: their inhabitants had died from starvation.

One story I remember was typical. Each day, while her mother went to search for wood along the edges of the forest Overvoorde, a neighbourhood girl, Johanna, cared for her siblings: a four-year-old brother and a weeks-old baby. Their father had been shipped off to a work camp in Germany. There was no gas and no electricity, and the water came on at one o'clock in the afternoon for only fifteen minutes. During this time it was Johanna's job to collect as much water as she could, in pails, pots, and pans, to be used later. It was a cold winter and with the baby in the crib, Johanna and her little brother would sit on the sofa wrapped in a blanket to keep warm. If they were lucky, they would have one slice of bread between the two of them, for the whole day—gummy, strange-tasting bread, half a loaf of which was the family's food ration for the week.

Johanna was only six years old. Her biggest fear was that her mother would not come home. Their mother, if not searching for wood, was out trading her possessions for sugar beets, tulip bulbs, and sometimes some dried beans. Johanna and her brother waited anxiously all day—and then, when their mother returned, there was the fright of the sleepless night, with bomber planes flying overhead. Fortunately, Johanna's father managed to escape from the work camp and, after the war, found his way back home.

It was good to be busy with playful things, because although the war was over, life was still a struggle. Many people had no work—the companies they had worked for were no longer in operation; factories and shops had been destroyed. There were no materials for manufacturing. Electricity was sporadic. Food was still hard to come by. We existed mainly on the food brought in by the Allies and the Red Cross. Fortunately, Folkert had found some work with the Canadian army, but it was occasional, doing some artwork for them whenever needed. He played in a band, too, that was hired from time to time for the entertainment of the troops. This brought in some funds to keep us going during these difficult times. Frey was kept fairly busy with her sewing work, mostly repairing and altering uniforms. Both of them often brought food home that had been given to them by the soldiers.

In the meantime, the black market racketeers were having a heyday, selling food and other much needed merchandise for exorbitant prices. The Dutch government decided to do some-thing about it. They announced that there would be a completely new currency, and set a date by which people had to change their old money for the newly designed bills and coins. If anyone came in with an unusually large amount of money, the government rea-soned, it would be confiscated if it could not be accounted for. It was a smart move, but the consequence was that the racketeers immediately turned their money back into goods they later could sell, receiving payment in the new currency. Some articles had become extremely desirable and could be sold for enormous sums of money: pianos, for example, and also motorcycles.

With our great financial stress, Mam was tempted to sell Pa's Harley-Davidson—it still sat, partially disassembled, in the *schuur*. But when she thought of Pa's disappointment when he returned, she couldn't do it. Underlying her reluctance was the unspoken idea that selling the Harley would be admitting that

Pa might not be coming back. "We'll see," Mam would say. "If there is absolutely no other solution, we'll do it." And then she would hesitantly add, "Pa probably wouldn't mind." So the decision would be postponed until the next crisis.

The other option was to sell our grand piano. But that would greatly disappoint Folkert, and after all, the piano was the reason he was playing in a band and earning us some income. So that possibility was also put on the "maybe" list.

Dick's father had returned from the German work camp, but he was in bad health and Dick and Mrs. van Duin feared the worst. Tonny was worried too. His older brother had also been taken by the Germans and had not been heard from since. Tonny and his family feared that, like so many others, he had not been able to survive the terrible conditions that prevailed in those camps.

Each one of us had a dark cloud hanging over his head. The tin boat project was a distraction, a way to stop thinking, if only momentarily, about the tragic problems that were gnawing away at our souls.

We began by collecting the empty tins from the portico and our apartments. We lined them up in different configurations, until Tonny came up with a pontoon arrangement: two rows of eight, connected with one tin at each end in between the rows. The idea was to sit at the back, on the tin that connected the aft end, and power the thing by putting our legs in the water and kicking.

We had set up our project downstairs in the portico. Folkert came by and asked what we were doing. When we told him, he considered the arrangement of the tins for a while. He pointed out what we already suspected—the clumsy craft would not be very buoyant, especially with all the weight concentrated on that one spot. And how were we going to attach the tins together?

He scratched his head and said, "I think that this stuff might solder. If you cut up some tins you can use the plating to join the tins together." He came up with lots of other good ideas—but it soon became obvious that we needed many more tins. Off we went, combing the neighbourhood. Soon we had more than we could carry. We stacked them under the staircase in the portico until the place was full. Fortunately, the neighbours didn't complain.

My father had taught me how to solder. The procedure was to heat a soldering iron, dip the hot iron into acid which was in a shallow dish with a copper penny in it, and then melt the soldering material onto the metal parts that were to be connected. We had soldering material, acid, and a penny. We had a soldering iron, too, but there was a problem. We usually soldered in the kitchen, where we could heat the iron on the stove. How were we going to heat the iron in the portico? There was no source of heat. After some searching we found a small one-burner kerosene stove in the *schuur*. To our surprise, next to it was a can of kerosene. How had they remained undiscovered when people were so desperate for cooking fuel?

We started cutting some of the tins, slicing the sides into strips of a width adequate to allow us to join two tins together.

I still wasn't quite sure we were going about it the right way. Putting the tins together in the upright position would be difficult because of the rounded corners. It would be better if we could put them down on their sides and attach the top and bottom ends together. But that would put the lid in the water, and if the lids leaked, water would run into the tins. Dick came up with a solution. "We have some cans with old paint," he said. "It is quite thick and gummy; if we put this around the edges of the opening and then squeeze the lid back on, wouldn't that seal it?"

"Yes, of course," said Tonny. "I bet that would do the trick." I agreed and we promptly got the paint, sealed one of the lids, and pushed the tin under the water. It didn't leak!

We worked on our biscuit-tin boat for many days. Often we were watched by other kids who had heard about our adventure.

There was no shortage of willing and helping hands. Soon we learned that we were not the only ones building a watercraft from tins. Other kids had started too.

When we finally launched our boat, it was a success. We soon found that it was easier to move forward with a short paddle than by treading with our feet. We would sit on one of the tins connecting the two pontoons, legs spread out wide, one on each pontoon, and wield the paddle in the water between the pontoons.

We built two more, so that we each had our own biscuit-tin boat. They attracted lots of interest from bystanders, and soon we couldn't even count the various versions of tin watercraft plying the waters of the Beek and the Laak. I even spotted one that accommodated four paddling kids.

We were proud of our accomplishment and I knew my father would be proud too. But where was he?

23

Weeks later, we still hadn't heard from Pa. Postal services were now getting back to normal and we hoped to receive word from him soon. Not a day went by that we didn't run to the door as soon as we heard the mailman putting something through the slot.

On June 28, 1945, again we heard the snap of the mail slot. Mam ran to the door, paused, then screamed. Frey and I ran to the door and there was Mam, sitting on the floor by the door holding a small piece of paper in her hand. "It's from Pa!" she yelled. "From Pa! He's alive!" Excited, we looked over her shoulders to read the letter.

It wasn't actually a letter. It was a small card with a printed message on one side, headed "Displaced Persons." Underneath was written, in my father's handwriting, Mam's name and our address. On the other side were preprinted sentences with tick boxes beside them, filled in and signed by my father. Mam handed it to Frey. We could now both take a good look at it.

DO NOT ALTER OR ADD TO THE PRINTED MESSAGE
Mark the sentences below thus: √

Dear *Alida*

√ I am well and safe.

√ Will write as soon as possible.

√ Expect to be home soon.

Do not write.

FOR ADDRESS ONLY
SEULEMENT L'ADRESSE
UITSLUITEND VOOR ADRES

TO
A
AAN

Mvr de Groot
moerweg 162

The Hague
Holland

CA/a18

DO NOT ALTER OR ADD TO PRINTED MESSAGE
NE RIEN CHANGER NI AJOUTER AUX MESSAGES IMPRIMES
VERANDER NIETS OF VOEG NIETS TOE AAN HET GEDRUKTE BERICHT

Date
Datum ___23.6.45___

Mark the sentences below thus: ☑   Cocher les phrases ci-dessous ainsi: ☑

Dear_____: Cher_____:

☐ I am well and safe.   ☐ Je suis sain et sauf.
☐ Will write as soon as possible.   ☐ J'écrirai dès que possible.
☐ Expect to be home soon.   ☐ J'espère revenir bientôt.
  Do not write.   N'écrivez pas.

Signature _____   Signature _____

Merk onderstaande zinnen met een merkteeken: ☑

Beste_____:

☑ Ik maak het goed en ben veilig.
☑ Zal zoo spoedig mogelijk schrijven.
☑ Verwacht gauw thuis te zijn.
  Schrijf mij niet.

Handteekening _____

We didn't quite know what to think of it. In a way it was a bit unnerving receiving such a short message; why had he not written a normal letter? On the other hand, it clearly stated that he was okay and would be home soon. A faint stamp on the paper indicated that it had been sent from Oranienburg, Germany. It had been mailed on June 23, 1945.

We read the message over and over again. I must have read it a thousand times.

"Mam," I said, "he wrote this on the twenty-third. If he left at the same time he could walk in anytime."

"Yes," said Mam, "I believe so too. Can't wait to tell Folkert!"

Every morning we expected to see Pa coming home that day. Each time the doorbell rang, we jumped up, hoping it would be Pa. Each time it was a disappointment. As the days went by, a shadow started falling over us. We scrutinized the message, speculations surfacing. Had someone else sent it? Was it a nasty joke? No—it was definitely Pa's handwriting.

In the middle of July, the doorbell rang again. As usual we jumped up and ran to the door, expecting to see Pa. Instead, there stood two men and a woman who looked familiar. Suddenly we recognized her. It was our former houseguest Lena.

"Lena," said Mam. "How are you?"

"I'm fine," she answered. "I'm here to get back my fur coat."

"Your what?" Mam asked, puzzled.

"You know, the coat that you stole from me."

Mam didn't know what to say. Suddenly one of the men stepped forward and introduced himself. "We are detectives with the police force," he said, "and are here to repossess a fur coat which this lady claims you stole from her when she was staying in your house during the occupation."

"Lena," Mam said, looking from her to the detectives and back again, "what on earth is going on here? You know I didn't steal a fur coat from you." Mam began to get agitated. "Haven't you done enough harm already? You betrayed everyone: my husband spent almost two years in a German concentration camp, and we had to escape to Friesland. He still isn't back; we don't know what has happened to him. What are you up to now?"

"I didn't betray anyone," Lena answered. "I'm here to get my fur coat. You stole it from me."

"Yes, you did betray us; you know that very well, and I can prove it. You called the SS after Isaac was arrested."

"Yes," Lena now said, "and that was your fault too."

One of the detectives saw how angry my mother was becoming. "Okay, calm down, ladies; we are not here to start an argument." He turned to Lena and said, "Would you recognize your fur coat if you saw it?"

"Of course," said Lena, "and I know where she keeps it too."

"Okay then, madam." Now turning to Mam, he said, "Could we come in and take a look at that coat?"

"Be my guest," said Mam, stepping aside. "Go ahead and get it, if you know where it is."

Lena pushed past her and went straight for the hall closet. She pulled out Mam's "fur coat." It was actually a coat with a fur collar and fur trim along the edges at the front and bottom. She had had it for years, since well before the war. "Here it is," Lena said with a satisfied smirk on her face.

"That's my coat," said Mam.

"No, it isn't; it's mine."

The detectives looked from Mam to Lena. The difference between the two women was obvious—Mam was tall and slender, and Lena was the complete opposite.

"I think we can settle this dispute, ladies," one of the detectives said. He asked Lena to put the coat on. Lena stuffed her arms through the sleeves with difficulty, and when she somehow managed to wriggle her body into the coat the front didn't close, and the hem of the coat was hanging over her feet.

The detectives could hardly manage to keep straight faces. One of them looked away, covering his mouth with his hand. The other detective said to Lena, "Madam, I don't think this is your coat."

"Yes, it is," answered Lena with authority.

"Well, if that is so, how come it doesn't fit?"

"Because she altered it," Lena said, pointing at Mam.

"Well, that is a possibility," said the patient detective, "and I can see how that might have made the coat narrower. But how was it made longer?"

For a moment Lena didn't know what to say, then she sputtered, "The pieces she cut to make it tighter have been used to make it longer."

"Oh, I see," said the detective. "Would you take it off, please, so we can take a closer look at it?"

With great difficulty Lena managed to peel the coat off her short, thick body. "Here you are," she said, handing the coat to the detective.

Both detectives took a good look at the coat. By this time Frey had arrived on the scene. "If you want to check for alterations, you will have to remove some of the lining," she said. "I'm a seamstress and I can do that for you, if that's okay." She looked at Mam.

"Yes, yes, go ahead," said Mam.

"I'll put it back together again afterwards," Frey assured Mam. Frey left, to return with a small pair of scissors. She loosened the lining from the bottom of the coat and rapidly exposed the inside. "Look," she said, "this is all one piece of fabric. Nothing has been added to make it longer. Also, if you look at the fur trimming, you can see that the flow of the texture and the blend of the colour variations are compatible with the rest. This is how it was made originally. It has not been altered." Both detectives nodded in agreement.

Lena, who almost had her nose buried into the exposed areas of the coat, suddenly said, "Well, then, where is my coat? What did you do with it?"

"I have no idea," Mam said. "Are you sure you had a fur coat? And is there anything else that I might have stolen from you? Your shoes, maybe? Or your brain?"

"Come," the detective said to Lena, "I think you have done enough harm here." He turned to Mam and said, "I apologize, madam. We run into this sort of thing every once in a while, and we have to follow up." To Frey he said, "Thank you very much for your help, but it was quite obvious from the beginning that we were on the wrong track. Again, our apologies to both of you." They grabbed Lena's arm and shoved her out the door.

Three months have passed since Vader's brief message without one further word from him. What is keeping him? Why is it taking so long?

On September 28, 1945, our questions are answered. Moeder and I are home alone. A man comes to our door. He introduces himself as Father van Kroon. He is a priest with the Roman Catholic Church. He asks us to let him in. We enter the living room and sit down. He tells us he knows Vader and unfortunately has come to bring us some bad news.

Moeder says, "Bad news? What kind of bad news? Is he held up somewhere? We've been wondering why it is taking so long for him to come home. Is he ill?" I snuggle up to Moeder. We are both sitting on the sofa, the priest across from us in a chair. Moeder puts her arm around me. We're both very worried. What could have happened now?

The priest shakes his head. "I'm sorry. There's no easy way to say this, but I have come to offer you my condolences. Dear lady, and you, his son"—he looks at Moeder and then at me—"your husband, your father, has passed away; he has joined our Lord in heaven."

Moeder and I are perplexed. What is this man saying? Moeder looks at him, shaking her head. "But that's impossible," she says.

"We received a note from him. He said he was okay, that he would be home soon. You must be mistaken. You must have him mixed up with someone else."

"I'm afraid not, ma'am. I was there when he died."

"No, no, no!" says Moeder, her voice rising. "I don't believe you." She stands up and walks around the room, her hands on her head, her fingers running through her hair. I don't know what to say. I sit on the sofa staring at Moeder. I feel numb and detached. This is not happening to us. I'm dreaming. Soon I'll wake up. I'm thinking about the tin boats. My *kano*, yes, my *kano*—tomorrow I must remember to get Dick and Tonny to help me get it out of the *schuur* and back into the Beek; we should go for a sail. It moves much better through the water than those tin boats.

The priest is talking again. I'm not really listening, just picking up a few words here and there. Vader was freed by the Russians. He weighed only thirty-four kilograms when they found him. The priest was there. They didn't know what to do with him; he was too weak to travel. They fed him and he started to improve a little. They decided to move him to Lübeck, to the American sector—there was a hospital there. But he was too weak. He died during the transport.

I get up and go to my room. I lie down on my bed and stare at the ceiling. I hear the door close; the priest is leaving. I hear Moeder sobbing. Why is she crying? Why does she cry? She cries because my father is dead. He has gone to the Lord, the priest told us. That means he is dead. My father is dead. Dead. He died! He is not coming home. Never! He will never come home. I will never, ever see him again. I have no father anymore. My father is dead, dead, dead; I will never see him again. A sob wells from my chest, tears start pouring from my eyes, I bury my head in the pillow and cry, my fists pounding on the mattress.

24

I cried for a long time. Then I turned onto my back and stared at the ceiling again. I didn't really see anything, just stared into space. I must have been in that position for hours. Suddenly I heard someone pounding on my bedroom door.

It was Folkert. "Jan, open the door." I must have locked it, couldn't remember. Again, "Jan, open the door. Let me in." It was Folkert again. I got up off the bed, but when I stood on the floor I almost collapsed. My legs were weak, almost too weak to stand on. Shaking and trembling, I finally made it to the door and turned the key. When Folkert stepped in, I sank down on the floor and just sat there. Folkert picked me up and said, "Come on, little brother, you can't stay in here forever." He carried me into the living room, where Frey and Mam were sitting, and put me down in a chair. On top of a table stood a small suitcase. It had been left there by the priest and belonged to my father. It was open and contained presents, among them two books marked "for Jan"—he knew I liked reading—and an electric razor "for Folkert." How he had been able to find and get those items, we would never know.

In October, we received a letter from the Red Cross confirming that my father had died in a hospital in Lübeck. The letter was dated October 18. His actual date of death was July 15, 1945.

All that time when we had been waiting and hoping...already then, Pa had been no more.

INFORMATIEBUREAU VAN

HET NEDERLANDSCHE ROODE KRUIS

~~CENTRAAL INFORMATIE EN CORRESPONDENTIEBUREAU. — MARKT 8, EINDHOVEN~~

No. IC1/14819
Bijlagen:

'S-GRAVENHAGE, 18 October 1945
~~EINDHOVEN~~ BENOORDENHOUTSCHEWEG 7
183450/54
Bij beantwoording dagteekening en nummer
van dit schrijven aan te halen.

Betreft:

Familie de Groot,
Moerweg 168,
's-GRAVENHAGE   *by Frontehnkade*

        Tot mijn diep leedwezen rust op mij de droeve
plicht U hierdoor mede te deelen, dat bij mijn Bureau een bericht
is binnengekomen omtrent het overlijden van den Heer
        Folkert de Groot, in het Hospitaal te Lübeck.
        Eventueel zou Kapelaan Kroon, wonende Berken-
boschblokstraat 19, Scheveningen, nadere inlichtingen kunnen ver-
strekken, daar hij destijds in het hospitaal te Lübeck wekzaam was.
        Ik wil niet nalaten U namens het Nederlandsche
Roode Kruis de verzekering te geven van mijn medeleven met dit voor de
nabestaanden zoo droevig verlies.

                        De fgd.Directeur,

                        (J.van de Vosse)

TYP/CJCB/AB
COLL.

K 855

The letter from the Red Cross confirming that my father had died in a
hospital in Lübeck.

An organization had been formed to provide financial assistance to those who had suffered losses caused by the war. I believe it was financed by the new German government. The organization was known as Stichting 40–45. Mam applied for help but was refused, probably because Pa had not belonged to the Dutch Resistance. She wondered what to do, how to make ends meet. Various plans were discussed. One thing she was sure of was that she did not want to stay in our apartment anymore: too many memories. "It's time to get on with our lives," she said.

From one of my aunts she heard that there was a large house for rent in Putten. Putten was a village in Gelderland, a picturesque province with large forests and heather-covered moors, much visited by tourists. I remembered the story Sjaak had told about what happened there after a failed attack by the Dutch Resistance.

"The house has eight bedrooms. It is on the outskirts of the village and bordered by a large forest," my aunt told us. Mam thought that it might be suitable for a small hotel or a bed and breakfast. She decided to investigate and went with my aunt to Putten. When she came back, she was full of enthusiasm. "It's a beautiful place," she said, "perfect for our purpose. I have rented it and we are moving in next month."

Folkert and Frey decided to stay in The Hague. They moved in with friends and Mam and I went to Putten. I missed my friends and Folkert and Frey, but I liked our new home. We named it 't Woudhuis (House of the Woods).

Things were getting back to normal; we began to carry on with our lives. But the war had left its marks everywhere. When school started, I discovered that only two kids in the entire place still had a father. Back in The Hague, Dick's father had not survived, and neither had Tonny's brother.

But we were lucky. Mam's business went well. After a few years she managed to buy the house. Mam even remarried, and

I acquired a stepfather—a very nice man whom I called Oom (Uncle).

Folkert and Frey married but later divorced. I became a merchant mariner. On one occasion my ship took me to Canada, that country to which our family still felt such a close connection. I was so impressed with it, I suggested to my brother he leave Holland and move there. He and his second wife emigrated to Canada in 1953. I followed in 1957, and my mother and stepfather joined us in 1958.

After everything that had happened, we were happy and proud to call ourselves Canadians.

Epilogue

After the war, many men claimed to have been active in the Resistance. Such claims have to be taken with a grain of salt. As is now clear, not everyone was active in the Resistance, and even of those who were, not all were heroes. Without a doubt, however, the soldiers of the Allied forces *were* heroes: those Canadians and Americans who went to fight a war when there was no selfish gain. They sacrificed their limbs and lives just to help and liberate others who were in a desperate situation. They themselves, their own countries, faced no immediate threat; they did not have to go to war. Yet they came! To me, the Canadian soldiers especially were heroes, because it was they who formed the main force that rescued the people of Holland.

What brought Europe to war at that time? Was it all because of an egotistical maniac, a failed painter named Adolf Hitler? I find it hard to believe that this lowlife would have been able to rise to such a powerful position without help from people with influence and money. There is plenty of money to be made in warfare. The German steel magnate Alfried Krupp, whose company helped arm the Nazis, was convicted at Nuremberg for using forced labour—but who were all the others, one wonders.

Was it the timing? Shortly before the war, the world economy was struggling—we had just gone through the Great Depression. Was it time to boost the automobile industry by building tanks and other army vehicles; to increase manufacturing and provide jobs by building warships and planes? A culture building for war needs the help of people willing to do terrible deeds. In the SS and the Gestapo, Hitler cultivated special troops consisting of bullies and rednecks, those types who in the normal course of life might not have accomplished anything. Even the regular German military were intimidated by them. With such a combination of culprits in power, it's no surprise that such horrific events became possible.

This combustible mixture of maniacal leadership, economic factors, and social pressures—the fuel that feeds the fire that cooks up war—can occur at any time in any nation, amid any race. It is happening today in the Middle East. Another one is simmering in the pot in North Korea, almost ready to be served. Every TV news flash of the parading army in North Korea shows a bone-chilling resemblance to the goose-stepping soldiers of the Nazi regime.

Wars have been waged since the beginning of time. In the early days we fought with stones and sticks, then with swords and spears. Now we are much more sophisticated and use bullets, bombs, and nuclear weapons. Will we ever learn? I am typing this into a computer, a clever machine that enables people all over the world to talk like neighbours. How is it possible that despite all our present knowledge, when it comes to dealing with other groups we still revert to the instincts and habits of the Stone Age?

In his letter of May 21, 1944, my father wrote: "People hate each other and they don't even know why." I think that sums it up. We find all sorts of reasons to treat with suspicion people of a nationality, religion, race, or colour different from our own. Yet they are people just like us, people who have the same hopes and needs. We are too afraid, or too greedy or lazy, to share, learn, and discover what we have in common. Instead, we fight: we kill one another, no different from our cave-dwelling forefathers.

I ask again: will we ever learn? You will be part of the answer.

Letters my father sent from the concentration camp at Vught, Holland, in 1944.

A Guide to Pronunciation

Here is a guide to pronouncing some of the Dutch terms and place names mentioned in the book. Look at the front of the book for pronunciations of characters' names.

bedstee (bed built into cupboard): "BED-stay"

Beek: "bake"

Beertje: roughly "BEAR-chuh"

Deventer: "DAY-vunter"

Friesland: "FREEZE-lont"

Gelderland: "HELD-erlont" (the *H* here means a kind of guttural sound like clearing your throat)

Groningen: HRO-ning-uhn (*H* is the clearing-throat sound)

Hadewiech Straat: "HAD-uh-weech straht" (The *ch* at the end of the first word is the clearing-throat sound; the *r* in the second word is slightly rolled)

(The) Hague: in Dutch, this is spelled den Haag and pronounced "den HAHG" (with the clearing-throat sound at the end)

Heerenveen: "HERE-uhn-VANE"

honger oedeem (swollen belly from hunger): "HOHNG-er oo-DAYM"

IJssel: "EYE-sul"

Joure: "YOW-ruh"

Kaag: "KAHG" (with the clearning-throat sound at the end)

kano (kayak-like boat): "KA-no" (the *a* sound isn't quite like the one in "cap" or "cop," but somewhere in between)

klompen (wooden shoes): "KLOHM-pen"

knikkers (marbles): "k-NICK-ers" (pronounce the *k* at the beginning)

koekjes (cookies): "KOOK-yuhs"

Koninkrijk der Nederlanden: "KONE-in-KRIKE dare NAY-derlahnden"

Laak: "Lack" (the *a* sound as in *kano*)

Leeuwarden: "LAY-wahr-den"

Marechaussee: "MAHR-uh-show-SAY"

Moerweg: "MOOR-wech" (clearing-throat sound at the end)

Nijmegen: "NYE-mech-un" (clearing-throat sound for the *ch*)

parlevinker (grocery boat): "PAR-levinker"

plantsoen (small park): "plahnt-SOON"

Putten: "PER-ten" (without pronouncing the *R*)

razzia (raid): "RAH-zee-ah" (slightly rolled *R*)

Rijssen: "RIYE-zen" (slightly rolled *R*)

Rotterdam: ROTE-ur-dahm (slightly rolled *R*)

Scheveningen: "SCHEY-ven-ing-en" (clearing-throat sound for the *CH*—not easy!)

schuur (storage shed): "schewr" (clearing-throat sound for the *ch*)

sloot (irrigation ditch): "slote"

't Woudhuis: "uht WOWD-how-uhs"

tover ballen (ball-shaped candies): "toe-ver BAHL-luhn"

Vught: "vercht" (without quite pronouncing the *r;* the *ch* is the clearing-throat sound)

Zuiderpark: "ZI-derpark" (long *I* sound after the Z)

Zutphen: "ZERT-phen" (without pronouncing the *R*)

zuurkool met spek (sauerkraut with bacon): "ZEWR-kohl met speck"

Zwolle: "ZWOLE-luh"

Acknowledgements

I have so many people to thank for getting my story in print that I hardly know where to begin. The events I have recorded, even though they happened a long time ago, are still vividly embedded in my memory and will likely stay that way forever. In putting my story on paper I had problems with dates, distances, and duration of time. When did this occur and how long did it last? Then I realized that time and distance seem completely different to a child than they do to an older person. After all, one year in the life of a seven-year-old is a full one-seventh of his or her lifespan, whereas one year for a seventy-year-old is one-seventieth. The same applies to distance and size. Einstein's theory of relativity is proved once again! I therefore have to thank first my cousins Mieke and Kees Harmsen who drove me on numerous occasions throughout the Netherlands to retrace routes and find locations and places that were important to the narrative. And Sandy, for her comments after patiently reading each page of the manuscript as it was written. I also must thank Nettie van der Putten for helping me with research, and the hundreds of readers of *De Krant* who responded to my desperate need for information on certain subjects. The response was overwhelming and it would take a separate book to mention all their names, but I do want to mention Hendrika Peeters-de Ronde, Dr. Hiltje Irausquin, Alice de Lorm, Ineke van Werkhoven (who paints beautiful watercolours), John de Vries, Jacoba van Dam-Bessey, Ed Nadort, Julie

Deutekom, Hanna Carp-Schipper, Jonina Potijk…but now I don't know where to stop. So many to thank; please forgive me if your name isn't mentioned here. One thing became clear: each Dutch man and Dutch woman who lived through wartime has a story to tell. Each one of us was living under terrible circumstances and had to overcome many difficulties to survive.

Writing a book is like building a musical instrument, which, providing it is well built, does not produce a good sound until it is finely tuned. Just like the tuning of an instrument, a book needs to be edited. I was lucky to have two of the best editors one could hope for: Laura Peetoom and Dawn Loewen. They both have perfect pitch and have done a tremendous job in tuning my manuscript. Then, last but not least, there is Diane Morriss, the publisher of Sono Nis Press. She has been extremely helpful with her enthusiasm and encouragement to get this book to press and with putting me in contact with those two awesome editors.

The author with Freya, his faithful companion.

Jan de Groot was born in 1932 in The Hague, Holland. He lived through the German occupation of Holland in the Second World War, and later, at the age of eighteen, he became a merchant mariner and roamed the world by sea. In 1957 he emigrated to Canada and in 1960 married a young Dutch woman who had also emigrated to Canada. They had two children, and Jan pursued a landlubbing career for thirteen years in the corporate world. In 1970, he returned to a seagoing life and operated a charter yacht in the Caribbean until 1980, divorcing and remarrying along the way. Jan is a certified master of seagoing vessels, and upon his return to Canada in 1980 he became a marine surveyor, inspecting ships and yachts for prospective purchasers, banks, and insurance companies.

Jan is now a widower and lives in Langley, B.C. He regularly contributes articles to boating magazines, and he writes for *De Krant*, a Dutch newspaper distributed throughout the world mainly to Dutch emigrants. He has also self-published *Buying the Right Boat*, a how-to book for yachting enthusiasts, and two books about his adventures in the Caribbean, *No Shoes Allowed* and *Gone to Come Back*. His next project is *The Ghost of the Ship Raven*, a true story about a ship that, possessed by a ghost, foundered on an uncharted reef near Haiti.